UNSAVORY THOUGHTS

THOMAS WALTON

Sagging
Meniscus

Cover: *Portrait of Blaise Pascal*, acrylic paint on paper, 2024, Douglas Miller.

Set in Mrs Eaves with LaTeX.

ISBN: 978-1-963846-28-7 (paperback)
ISBN: 978-1-963846-29-4 (ebook)
Library of Congress Control Number: 2025930087

Sagging Meniscus Press
Montclair, New Jersey
saggingmeniscus.com

"I condemn equally those who choose to praise man, those who choose to condemn him and those who choose to divert themselves, and I can only approve of those who seek with groans."

—Blaise Pascal

"The story of my life does not exist. It is not to tell my story that I write. Writing has taken from me what was left of my life. It has emptied me and I no longer know what—in what I have written about my life—is real, and what I actually experienced."

—Marguerite Duras

CONTENTS

DANIIL KHARMS MADE ME DO IT

THAT SHALLOW BROOK

UNSAVORY THOUGHTS

Do Not Read Prefaces

"In every book the preface is the first and also the last thing. It serves either to explain the purpose of the work or to justify it and answer criticism. But readers are generally not concerned with moral purposes or with attacks in reviews, and as a result, they do not read prefaces. It is a pity that this is so. Our country is still so young and naïve that it fails to understand a fable unless it finds a lesson at its end. It misses a humorous point and does not feel irony: it simply is badly brought up."

So begins Mihail Lermontov in his masterful preface to his novel, *A Hero of Our Time*. Lermontov is writing in 1840, and *A Hero* arrives at the beginning of what will be the golden age of Russian Literature (Pushkin's *Eugene Onegin* precedes *A Hero* by a few years, Gogol's *Dead Souls* appears two years later, in 1842, Turgenev and Tolstoy start to publish in the 1850s, and Dostoevsky in the 1860s). Lermontov's preface reads as if it could've been written today. Our own reading public, art-going public, and, well, general public, has hardly become more sophisticated. In fact, over the last two hundred years our ability to read well (closely, with nuance and a recognition of irony) has gotten worse. And in this century, things have gotten *much worse*. Willfully worse.

This book, *Unsavory Thoughts*, is a persona poem, a satire, a collection of irony-laced pastilles. This will be lost on many. Even though I have just said it, explicitly. We are living in a literal age. We take ourselves very seriously. We are sincere and unamused by amusement.

Lermontov again: "Our public resembles a provincial who, upon over-hearing the conversation of two warring Courts, is convinced that each envoy is betraying his government in the interests of a most ten-der mutual friendship. The present book has only recently suffered from the unfortunate faith that certain readers and even certain re-viewers have in the literal meaning of words. With us the most fantas-tic of all fairy tales would hardly escape the reproach of being meant as some personal insult."

Sound familiar? Our audiences seem all too eager to claim per-sonal insult. We willingly ignore irony, satire, and parody. We are fierce literalists. Taking offense is what validates us, and places us firmly on the right side. For to be righteous, is to be aggrieved.

We are all familiar, I think, with the myth that began in the 19th century, that we homo sapiens use only 10 percent of our brains. Let's assume it's true, and that in Lermontov's time we only used one-tenth of our brains. It would seem to me that in our time we surely use less. In fact, we go out of our way to allow technologies to think for us. We outsource our brains. We are addicted to convenience and the hack. Designed obsolescence used to mean a product that was intentionally built to become obsolete in the not-too-distant future. It now seems to mean products that are designed to make *us* obsolete in the not-too-distant future. What laze is this? Where have all the luddites gone?

Whatever can be delivered to us, we sign up for enthusiastically. Whether that be our groceries or our ideas, our robot vacuum cleaner or our political opinions. The goal for most of us seems to be to think and do as little as possible. As if that were some sort of genius, and only fools (and the poor) would stoop to do anything for themselves. Every day without fail, I have seen out my window my neighbors be-ing brought a single cup of coffee and a pastry. Sometimes the deliv-ery driver is old, nearly unable to climb the front stairs of the brown-stone apartments on my block. Always, the car in which the driver has arrived is clunky, dented, and growls as it pulls away. The neighbors never speak to their courier or say thank you. It is arranged to be a contactless interaction. In fact, not an interaction at all. An interaction would require a more vigorous use of the brain, some social skills, perhaps even some wit or empathy, etc. I often wonder what my neighbors are doing that's so important that it keeps them from walking half-a-block to the café down the street . . . I suppose they lead more interesting lives than I do.

Lermontov again: "You will say that morality gains nothing from this book. I beg your pardon. People have been fed enough sweetmeats; it has given them indigestion: they need some bitter medicine, some caustic truths. However, do not think the author of this book has the hope of reforming humankind. The Lord preserve him from such benightedness! He merely found it amusing to draw humankind as he found it, such as he has met it again and again. Suffice it to say, the disease has been pointed out; goodness knows how to cure us."

Here you are then: a little medicine to make us sick, a little poison to make us well.

I.

WRONGS OF PASSAGE

*In which the author realizes
he doesn't remember very much
about his childhood*

Two Truths and a Lie

> "Out of a hundred years a few minutes were made that stayed
> with me, not a hundred years."
> —Antonio Porchia

I don't think about my childhood very much. Or rather, I didn't think about my childhood very much, until I had a child myself. Like all new parents, during those first couple years I marveled as my daughter's unintelligible sounds turned into words, and then those words turned into a-syntactical collages, and then eventually, sentences. It happened quickly, in retrospect. And it seemed that as soon as she learned to form questions, she started asking me the same one nearly every night: "Papa will you tell me a story about when you were a little boy?"

I hadn't expected this to be part of parenting: reliving my childhood through storytelling. But for several years she asked, and nearly every night for several years it was a challenge for me to come up with something new, a task made all the more difficult as I realized that I didn't remember very much. Almost nothing. Almost nothing when you consider an entire childhood. Eighteen years of my life reduced to a few dozen memories. I was shocked to find how few stories I remembered. The ones I could remember were mostly vague and incomplete. Impressions, I guess, of memories. Something like how in a Monet painting of water lilies everyone can see that the flowers depicted are water lilies even though they don't really look like water lilies at all. I found that the "memories" I had of my childhood were little more

3

than images that lacked the narrative elements to be properly called a "story." My daughter wanted stories, but my memories were merely impressions—water lilies, rotting apples, flags blowing on a beach—not stories at all.

Some things, though, came back to me quickly and nearly complete. Like the time we were sledding up at the water tower. I was probably five or six, and our neighbor Mike Bell gave me a wedgie so violent he ripped my underwear to shreds. My oldest sister was there. She had a crush on him. She watched the whole thing happen. She laughed and walked away with him. I walked home alone, with a plastic sled under my arm. I never forgot that, nor forgave her for not defending me. Forty-odd years after the fact, I confess, though I'm not mad about it, I still haven't forgiven her. I realize it's ridiculous. I suppose it's a kind of scar.

Other stories came as I started telling them, as if I was spelunking, searching for them with the very words I was using to tell them. I remembered them as I went, as I told them. Like the time we all went ice skating at Scout Lake, in Milwaukee. My mom, my little brother, my two sisters and I. I didn't skate well, but I'd been to hockey games, so I learned to imitate the players. I could skate fast, and stop on a dime. It wasn't graceful. It was more like running than skating, but it was fun, I guess, for me. My brother was the same. We would skate around the lake trying to knock each other over—not difficult it turns out. Sometimes we carried sticks and used a tin can as a hockey puck, but the game was mostly about knocking the other person down.

My mother, on the other hand, was gifted. She had been a figure skater in her youth. She knew how to skate backwards and spin. She even performed a few jumps. She was pure grace on the ice, and when my brother and I got tired or hurt, we'd lie there on the frozen lake and watch her skate around us. I don't think we could articulate the concept of beauty yet, I'm not sure children are capable of that, but if we couldn't speak its name, we could certainly recognize it. We were mesmerized, confused. Huge snowflakes fell in slow unpatterned derivations. Her skates whisked along the ice as she spun herself into a blur, or glided through the flurry with an elegance that hypnotized us.

I don't remember my sisters skating. They were much older than my brother and me. Teenagers. I have a vague recollection of them drifting slowly around the lake, rolling their eyes at us and talking in whispers with their friends. Their friends—butterflies to our mere larval stage—may as well have been a species from another planet.

I admit that when I told my daughter that story over dinner, I embellished it with certain details. Details I didn't really remember, but must've felt: the sting of the cold on my cheeks as we lay there on the ice, my mouth open, trying to catch snowflakes on my tongue, my mother singing "It's Raining on Prom Night" as she skated around us, floating through the falling snow.

That never happened, exactly, but it's certainly not a lie.

THE BOY IN THE BARN

My father's father was, by all accounts, passive. A docile man universally loved. He was dominated by his wife who, to be fair, dominated our entire family. She was a master manipulator (who I loved, may she rest in peace). My father, an only child, could've probably put an end to her rather oppressive reign, but for whatever reason, failed to stand up to his mother. Not only that, he passed his unresolved issues with her onto us by either committing some of the same parental abuses himself, or correcting those parental abuses to such an extent that the corrections became abuses in and of themselves.

Perhaps "abuse" is too strong a word (I can hear my sister saying). My siblings and I dealt with the "situation" in various ways. In various ways rebelled, exploited, hid, or simply fled: the old comedy of masks.

One of the ways I dealt with the situation growing up was by getting myself thrown in jail. Indeed, I was the black sheep of black sheep. A black goat, maybe (with the mouth of a lion, and the hairy feet of a bear). Not that I was some sort of dangerous criminal. My jailtime was mostly for petty vandalism, underage drinking, malicious mischief, running from the cops. Like many teenagers, I fell under the spell of a nebulous rebellion, the swank of juvenile delinquency. One of my favorite pastimes was breaking the plate glass windows of fancy-looking banks. After being caught one night, I excused myself by telling my mother I couldn't resist the sound of shattering glass. Once I stole a carton of cigarettes from a grocery store outside of Chicago and spent four frigid January days and nights in jail. I lived on the street in New Orleans with my friend Jason (now dead). One night we were caught urinating on St. Louis Cathedral. We were promptly arrested, along with twenty or thirty other street kids loitering about. As the riot squad was loading us into paddy wagons, I was able to sneak away, then sprint away, and lose myself in the drunken chaos of Bourbon Street. In all, I was arrested five times, but that hardly represents my "arrestable offenses."

I don't mention all of this to brag. I say it because I don't really understand it. Or rather, I say it to try to understand it. To shine a light on it. I think I was raised (in an unspoken way) to break the rules, to resent the authorities, not to trust the government, the police and politicians. I wonder if my family has had a chip on its shoulder ever since we immigrated. Each branch of our family tree tinged with trauma and a vague mistrust of the other trees around. Certainly a mistrust of the taller trees. We were farmers, poor and poorly educated, proud, Scots Irish or Welsh or Welsh Irish or Scots or Irish Welsh Scots and yes please I'll have another. We broke our backs and slurred our words, what of it. We simultaneously resisted wealth and weirdly envied it.

I make the joke sometimes that yes, I'm a Walton, but not from the wealthy Walmart-empire Waltons or the anodyne goodnight-JohnBoy Waltons, I'm descended from the lesser-known line of horse-thief Waltons. I'm not ashamed of it. I'm not proud of it. It just is what it is. But what is it? I guess I'm trying to process it.

My father was an only child, but my mother had four brothers, all of whom were, essentially, salesmen. They sold cars or houses or insurance. If you needed it, they would sell it to you. In fact, they would sell it to you whether you needed it or not. One of her brothers, though, never matured into grift. Sadly, when he was in high school he got in a car accident and became paralyzed from the waist down, suffering brain damage. He spent the rest of his life (fifty-plus years) living with his parents, my grandparents. When we were kids, the three of them moved next door to us. My brother and I would go every day after school to their house, where my invalid uncle would shout from his chair, "lift me up!" My grandfather would curse, walk over to him, then reach his hand down my uncle's back and grab him by the belt to pull him up straight in the chair. I saw this happen thousands of times, and it never once occurred without a volley of curses thrown from father to son and back again. My brother and I learned how to swear from them. The curses flew like chicken feed around the room. Meanwhile, my grandmother played and sang hymns on an out-of-tune spinet piano next to my uncle's chair. The bread she made weighed a thousand pounds, but that didn't stop us from smothering it in gravy. That house was a rich mix of the sacred and profane.

My mother's father worked for eighteen years as an electrician for Union Electric in St. Louis. He was retired by the time I was born. I knew him as an old man, gruff, callous, always busy and always in a fight or argument with someone or some thing. The rooster in the chicken coop was his most consistent and formidable adversary. My grandfather's bald head was more often than not scratched and bloody. There wasn't a day we spent there that he didn't curse that rooster for attacking him. But he never killed it. He suffered his antagonist as if it were a penance.

Though Baptist, my maternal grandparents seemed to me essentially Pentecostal. When I got a tattoo, my mother's mother told me I now had the mark of the beast mentioned in Revelations (mouth of a lion, hairy feet of a bear) and I was surely going to hell.

"Well at least I'll have family there," I said.

She responded dismissively, "Pshaw pshaw."

I admit I've never felt comfortable around WASPS, or wealthy Catholics, or moneyed suburbanites. Not because I'm prejudiced, but because those people are foreign to me, well-adjusted, sophisticated, refined. They know how to set a dinner table and use the correct fork for dessert. Not only that, they have faith in society and cultural institutions in a way that I just don't understand. I can't. It's not in my skin to understand it. Not in my flesh. Not in my roots. Even now I feel like people who are well-adjusted are either highly medicated, extremely adept at self-deception, or mentally ill.

I feel the same way about MFA programs, which, like all 21st-century writers, I felt the need to attend. I made my attempt (if belated) to suffer grad school, but I just couldn't bear it. Regarding higher education, I'm more likely to get banned from a university than to be matriculated into one. My skin crawled during my time on campus, so much institutionalized dishonesty, elitism, and shoulder-rubbing going on. What a perfect little hideous bubble, one far too utopian for me. I'd rather be drinking cheap wine in the bushes off-campus than attending classes on one. I dropped out after a semester, got married and ran away with my new bride to Australia, and then Taiwan. The marriage lasted all of five years. Our daughter is now 18 and, ironically, about to go off to college.

If culture is (as my dictionary says) "the totality of socially transmitted behavior patterns, acts, beliefs, institutions, and all other products of human work and thought," then it's not necessarily a positive thing to be cultured. Nor can any one individual or group of individuals have *more* culture than the next. We are all cultured. We have no choice. Culture is imposed on us. It can be vibrant and delightful, or it can be terrible and destructive, humdrum and boring, materialistic, superficial, or full of elaborate rites and festivals. In every case, it is always culture. Or rather, in every case, it is only culture. I am inclined to think of culture in an anthropological sense. It's the sea in which we swim, and that swims in us. It's also the air we breathe and often do not see.

I recognize that my distrust of authority, intellectualism and polite society originates in the culture I grew up in. Originates with my family and their mistrust of all things other than, well, my family. It's a very odd and very sick snake that eats its own tail. Though weirdly not uncommon. We become saturated by our culture when we're young, and very seldom dry out completely. To transcend the culture in which we're raised would seem to me to require an act of Herculean strength. It would necessitate a change so complete that it would have to occur on a cellular level.

What's the saying? "You can take the boy out of the barn, but you can't take the barn out of the boy." Well (as my wife will attest), you can't take me anywhere. There's no politesse that can stand the residual stench of the barn in which I was raised.

Maculate Conception

I wasn't born anywhere.

I have a birth certificate, like anyone else, but what it says is confusing. Essentially that I was born on Friday the 13th at such and such a time in the year 1973 to Beverly J Holcomb and Wallace E Walton. I recognize the names of my mother and father, and the city—Milwaukee— but the birth certificate belongs to someone else. And those names— Beverly and Wallace—who are they now? Who were they then? We cannot be the same person twice, much less fifty years on. My mother was only twenty-seven when I was born. My father thirty. At thirty I was still on drugs, reading Rilke, wandering the flatirons of Colorado imagining I was in a castle in Duino. Hardly ready to be a father, though I would be soon thereafter, ready or not.

I wasn't born anywhere. It wasn't exactly a straightforward delivery. I weighed ten and a half pounds, and my mother says I was "black and blue all over. You looked like you'd been in a fight," I've heard her say a thousand times, "and lost."

The apartment my parents took me to in Milwaukee, after the hospital, on Root River Drive, I don't remember. I couldn't find it if I had to. I do remember the black-and-white TV, its grainy picture and the weird light it cast through the room. It was always dark in that apartment, in the early '70s.

I was born in the 1900s, the certificate says. The 20th century used to feel modern. I mean, modernism *happened* in the 20th century! In fact, it started in the 19th century! By mid-century, the 20th century came to feel futuristic, post-modern. With moon landings and space needles, *The Jetsons*, Mork from Orc and *Star Trek*. We had DeLoreans and robots, and vacuum cleaners that looked like robots . . . We were living in the space age of our imagination. We'd learned to fly, but not that cigarettes could kill us. We had cordless phones, but weren't as yet umbilicalized to them.

As I'm writing this, it's 2023, fifty years until 2073, when I will be 100. I'll soon be closer to 2073 than to 1973. What weird and wild, mind-numbing, sloth-producing, self-defeating technologies will we have then? What designed obsolescence? What divine putrescence? How far will God have sunk then? If we are to credit Descartes with having struck the first death blow, then it's been centuries already since we killed that poor bearded myth in the sky.

I wasn't born anywhere. Like an immigrant, my home too is imagined. First forgotten, then imagined. A figment rather than a certificate. An embellishment, a fantasia whose actuality is lost to time as well as place.

There was an era when children were born in the same house they would decades later die in. At least born in the same town they would die in. And they knew where they were born, could take you there and say, "see that house . . . that's where I was born and raised." But not anymore, not for a long time. I'm afraid the house is gone, torn down, abandoned. So now we merely imagine our birthplaces. We spin fantastic narratives about how wonderful it was before our parents moved us away from the place we were born to some other town, to some other town from which we'll most likely also grow to feel estranged.

I wasn't born anywhere, I don't live anywhere, and I won't die anywhere. I probably won't be buried anywhere either. Who gets buried anymore? They will carry me to the fire and turn me to ash. And I will drift away in a pointless breeze, that same or similar breeze from which I came.

My Brother, My Killer

When we were kids, my brother and I wrapped duct tape around whiffle balls and threw them at each other. The object was simple: hit the other in the face. Oh sure, we started out playing a proper whiffle ball game, but that game always devolved into war. And tears.

My brother had no sense of the ethics of war. He feigned ignorance of the Geneva Convention, or any other convention for that matter. War crimes to him were not taboo, but exercises in innovation. Over the years, he threw all kinds of things at me—whiffle balls, baseball bats, skateboards, hammers. He put the gorilla in guerilla warfare: in fact, if he'd had a gorilla, he would've thrown it at me.

Every whiffle ball contest (every contest of any kind, really) ended with him running into the garage and searching for something to launch at me. He usually missed. I was agile enough to avoid his attempts to murder me. It's surprisingly easy to dodge a hatchet thrown at you by a hysterical seven-year-old. Even if you are only nine.

He did connect on occasion, and I still have a few scars as evidence of his success. Once, an aluminum baseball bat spinning wildly through the air caught me in the knee. It didn't hurt so much as tingle. A shiverous vibrato played up and down my left leg.

The worst by far was the hubcap. The hubcap came whizzing toward me like a UFO, except that I knew the whole time it was a hubcap. It was an IFO. Or an IFH. Or just an FH, a flying hubcap.

I ran when I saw it coming, zig zagging to try to avoid its trajectory, but the FH's coordinates were locked in on me. No zig was zig enough, and no zag. The hubcap was single-minded, and caught me on the crown of my head. I fell, and then put my hand up to my head. I could feel the warm blood trickling down the back of my neck. There was a gash in my skull, a thick flap of skin had flipped up and filled with hair. It burned and bled and I could feel it throbbing.

That's the time, after the hubcap, that I'd had enough. I confess I beat my little brother to a pulp. I confess I derived a kind of sadistic pleasure from it. I confess that after the beating, I stuffed him in one of those plastic garbage bins that latch shut. I confess that I told him if he made a single sound, I would roll the garbage can into the hole where we dumped all the rotten apples and grass clippings, the hole we both knew was full of snakes and spiders and hornet nests.

"You better not make a sound," I said, and went inside.

An hour or so later, at dinner, we all sat down and started eating. My parents, my two older sisters and me.

"Where's your brother?" my dad said, with a tired expression.

I shrugged, "Don't know."

He turned his head away from the TV to look at me, "Go find him."

I went out to the garbage bin. There must've been holes in it that allowed for air to enter, because he was still alive. I unlatched the lid and opened it. He was trembling, and there were mud streaks under his eyes where the tears had run.

"Dinner's ready."

Edible Undies

We had a dog when I was a kid, but only briefly. It was the kind of dog that misbehaves. It chewed everyone's shoes up, chewed up our toys, raided the laundry and chewed my father's underwear. The dog was sick. Perverted. Obsessed. We got rid of it.

I never loved the dog or wanted it. I can't remember who did. It just showed up one day. That's how I remember it. Maybe Trish, my oldest sister. She fell in love easily, was whimsical, emotional. She had strong feelings about things. I can't remember if she was upset when my parents sent it back. Probably so, but I don't remember.

Sent it back where? I never knew. They just kept saying, my parents: "We'll have to send it back."

"No, don't send it back!" my brother cried, but he was the baby of the family and no one cared what he thought. Even now we don't care what he thinks. He's a forty-eight-year-old college professor of sociology with a PhD, and my family still doesn't care what he thinks.

I just watched the whole thing happen. That's just the way I was, I guess. I just watched things. My mother always said I was "observant." I suppose that's true. But I wasn't just neutrally observing things, I was watching things the way you might if you were in an operating theatre and some terrible botched surgery was taking place in front of you. When I say I just watched the whole thing happen, I mean the whole thing with the dog, but also everything else, too. It never made sense to me. None of it. It didn't make sense that day the dog was suddenly there, and it didn't make sense when they sent it back.

I don't remember caring, really, either way. I only wondered where they were sending it. Where do you send a dog that eats underwear?

No One Slams the Porchdoor Anymore

In the Pacific Northwest, thunderstorms are rare. It's been almost two years since we had a proper storm. September. A morning like this. I remember it well. I was reading a book about Isaac Newton. One of those revisionary histories where you find out it wasn't really Newton at all who discovered this or that, but someone else, someone else who's name (until this book) had been lost to obscurity.

That's the last time we had a thunderstorm around here. I know because I remember the dogwoods were just starting to turn reddish purple, like now. Just like they used to do in southern Illinois where my grandparents lived, where we went when we were kids. We would drive down from Milwaukee. The trip would take all day, the six of us in our panel wagon, not a seatbelt in sight. (I'm sure the old car had seatbelts, but no one ever used them. We thought of them as ornamental. Or something to play with when we got bored.) We'd have to leave early, before the traffic in Chicago got bad. If that happened, my father would curse the city and everyone who lived there. I was raised to hate Chicago, and only recently changed my mind. Old prejudices are hard to shake, and die a slow, ungraceful death.

My grandparents lived on a farm. Or rather, there was farmland all around where they lived, so it seemed like they lived on a farm. They had goats, and chickens, and those metal porch chairs that you could sort of rock in, or bounce in. Not a rocking chair, exactly, but a bouncing chair. And if you bounced it hard enough, the chair would move across the floor. My brother and I used to have races in them, or play "bumper chairs," much to the irritation of my grandmother, who told us we were "full of beans and busy as flies in a window screen."

There were always a few old dogs, tick-infested, asleep on the porch. The porch wasn't really a porch. It was a concrete slab outside the back screen door. More like a patio I guess, with a filthy, plastic, corrugated roof "overtop it" (that's how my grandma said it, "overtop it"). The screen door would slam shut and my grandma would yell at us to "stop slammin the porchdoor!" My grandma was a hard woman, and you didn't mess with her. But we were just kids. We couldn't help it. We bounced the chairs and slammed the doors, and threw rocks at the chicken coop, almost as if by accident, by fate. She would thwap us on the rump with a plastic fly swatter as she yelled, and we'd run outside, the door slamming behind us. "I said stop slammin the porch-door!"

That was forty years ago. More. And now the old dogs are dead, the ticks dead, my grandmother dead. And also the "damned rooster" that used to attack my grandfather's bald head when he went into the coop to gather eggs. The rooster's dead. My grandfather's dead. All of it dead. Even the farm itself is gone. My mother told me they plowed it all flat, filled in the creek where we used to drop stones from the bridge to crack the ice in winter. They bulldozed the old haunted shed we called the "ghostcow shed," the one we dared each other to go inside at night (no one ever did). All of it dead, all of it gone. The potato cellar where we sheltered during tornadoes, listening by candlelight to the old battery-powered radio, to see if it was safe to come out, to hear where the tornadoes were and where they were headed. How terrifying was that! A proper storm! Thunder cracking and rolling outside, jars of beets and green beans rattling on shelves all around us. We sat on huge sacks of potatoes listening to the wind howl and roar outside. And then, after an hour or so, going out, assessing the damage, making huge piles of limbs that had fallen from the tulip trees, the sassafras, and oaks. All dead. And the bonfire we lit the next day. Dead.

There's a subdivision there now. A subdivision where my grand-parents used to live, and their parents before them. A neighborhood full of sterile suburban houses in cul-de-sacs. A neighborhood full of newly rich folks from Carmi who watch endless amounts of TV, though they don't call it TV anymore. They watch "shows." They hire com-panies to mow the grass once a week, and have their groceries de-livered by people with less money than them. They sit in their over-stuffed reclining chairs and eat and drink (and think) what they're told, and can hardly be bothered to walk to the door to get the packages they've ordered online. It's a kind of afterlife, I guess. A post-ambulant age that's surrendered itself to the screen. A technocratic age where no one slams a porchdoor, there are no roosters, and no filthy kids to throw rocks through the already broken windows of old haunted sheds.

Uncle Glenard's Still

I am old enough to remember vague references to my great-uncle Glenard's still. My brother and I tried to find it every time we went down there, to my grandparents' farm in southern Illinois. We called it a farm but it wasn't. They just lived in the sticks. That's what my grandma called it, "the sticks."

My great-aunt said Glenard always kept to himself. He'd wander off for hours and nobody knew where he went. Sometimes he snuck out at night. She thought her brothers knew about the still, too, but didn't say anything because their parents were Bible-thumping teetotalers who thought that alcohol of any kind was the devil's work. They were right, of course—that's why we love it.

When Glenard was only twenty, he was accidentally shot while butchering hogs. The men in the family would run the pigs out of the barn into a kind of corral, and then they would shoot them. That's how they used to kill them. This time, tragically, as they were shooting them, Glenard got hit. The nearest hospital was in Carmi, twelve miles by wagon. My great-grandfather wrapped him in blankets and they started off. He died on the way. They came back to the house and laid him out on my great-grandparents' bed until the undertaker showed up. The undertaker embalmed him right there on the bed. I think about this sometimes. How his corpse, so recently alive, just lay there waiting for his coffin to arrive. How cold and quiet that night must've been.

Before leaving, the undertaker hung a wreath on my great-grandparents' front door.

And so began the legend of Uncle Glenard's still. He was the only one who knew where it was. If it ever was. And because he was now dead, the legend grew and grew.

I suppose they did farm some things. Everybody did around there. When my mother was a child, they had a sorghum mill. They made molasses. By the time I was born the cane fields had given way to corn and potatoes. A few stray sorghum grasses grew up every year along the tree line and beside the crick. That's what my grandma called it, "the crick."

We never found the still. The rumor was it was somewhere past the pond, just over the hill where the huge walnut tree grew. That walnut tree was cut in half by lightning one spring. My grandma said the resulting flash smelled of moonshine enough to make the whole county drunk, she said, "drunk as a tick on a hound dog's neck."

My brother and I searched everywhere for Uncle Glenard's still, but we never found anything. Our cousin said that he heard there was a trunk of buffalo nickels in it worth a fortune. Once we found a pet cemetery with a few stones laid conspicuously about. We started digging under the stones, thinking maybe the treasure was hidden with the dead pets, but after we found a burlap sack wrapped around a tangle of bones, we stopped digging there. We both felt sick, and we very carefully covered them back up.

Sometimes we just went to the walnut tree and acted drunk. We pretended we had big mason jars full of moonshine. We'd clink glasses and throw them back, and then stumble around and fall. My brother thought it was funny when I acted like I was vomiting.

We were just kids. We thought twenty was old. We thought someone who was twenty was an adult. We never thought of Glenard as a kid, as one of us. As being there with us while we stumbled around, or tripped over the frozen furrows and the shin-high stalks left from the previous year's corn.

IN A WILD WEST STYLE

When I was eight, my family moved from Milwaukee down to southern Indiana. The best thing about southern Indiana is leaving southern Indiana. Every summer we would travel up to central Michigan to spend a week at my great uncle's lake house. This was my father's side of the family. My father's father's brother. Central Michigan, to us, was a kind of Cote d'Azure, a sort of Midwestern Riviera. The network of lakes seemed more archipelago than lacustrine. We spent those summer days on innertubes leashed behind a speedboat racing through spent fireworks and empty beer cans adrift in the tepid, gasoline-heavy lake. A punishment we excitedly looked forward to.

Fine dining for us, in southern Indiana, was either a Mexican restaurant near the mall called Hacienda, or fried cheese sticks and pizza at the Darmstadt Inn. On rare occasions, we were allowed to have a "Kiddie Cocktail" or, for dessert, a Frosty. While summering in the Michigan Riviera, my father's parents treated the whole family, one night only, to The Golden Nugget Saloon. We were made to understand that this was a treat. This was elegance. The Golden Nugget Saloon was a faux Wild West kitsch restaurant in Michigan's Irish Hills. They had a taco Tuesday, a Friday night fish fry, and a Saturday Prime Rib special. My brother and I ordered hamburgers and fries no matter what day of the week.

The Golden Nugget Saloon also had a video game arcade that was in a train caboose smashed onto the side of the restaurant. You accessed it in the back of the dining hall by walking up a few stairs. The caboose was full of pinball machines, Ms. Pacman, Galaga, Donkey Kong, etc. It was heaven to us, that is, to my brother and me. We learned to stretch our quarter on the Ms. Pacman machine. The more points my heroine gobbled, the less time we had to spend at the table with our hands in our laps trying in vain to follow the meandering chatter of my grandmother's monologues, how "Vera Ellesburg had recently found a new hairdressers over near where the Sears was for years but is now not there of course because the Express Way changed all that . . . your grandfather and I still refuse to use that cursed road, isn't that right dear?" (Cue polite smile from grandfather.)

The nights at The Golden Nugget, like most other nights, usually involved a fight of some kind between my brother and me. Neither of us were ever to blame, of course. (Did we ask to be brothers? I think not.) This particular night, our fight would be blamed on the pinball machine.

After getting a few quarters from my grandfather, we spent a good ten minutes on Galaga and Ms. Pacman. Then switched to pinball. My brother wasn't tall enough to see the obstacle course, so I had to lift him up and hold him while he played. After I played the first ball, I grabbed him around the waist and lifted him as he pulled the spring back and shot the ball around the top of the machine. The ball leapt and shot and darted and bounced around, bells and whistles and flashing lights. My brother's eyes were wide as the shiny silver ball shot here and there and then quickly raced right between the flippers he flipped a full second after the ball had disappeared.

I dropped him then, and when I did his chin hit the glass edge of the machine. He bit his tongue and started screaming.

"What?" I said.

"My tongue!"

"Let me see."

When he opened his mouth a slug of blood spilled out and fell to the floor.

"Oh shit," I said.

"You dropped me!" he screamed and started throwing punches at me.

Because he was two years younger than I was, he wasn't really a threat in terms of strength, but he was extremely unpredictable and therefore dangerous. He fought like the Tasmanian Devil from the Looney Tunes cartoons. I had learned that my only defense was to get him in a bear hug and wrestle him to the ground, or to run, to outrun him until he got tired or just gave up.

This particular time, in The Golden Nugget Saloon, I got caught in between. I both grabbed him *and* ran. I failed to subdue him, and he whirled and spun and threw his fists out in a Tibetan drum of punches. One flew straight for my head, and I ducked, and when I ducked, I stumbled portside in the caboose and fell down the few stairs leading back to the dining hall. I crashed down the stairs and into a white-bloused waiter carrying a round tray full of mashed potatoes, prime rib and overboiled frozen vegetables. The waiter swerved, and when he did, the delicate balance of the tray was upset as he fell fast three steps to his right and dropped the whole thing with a crash onto an eight top. A loud shatter and a terrible splash of beverages ensued, startled screams and chairs pushed back.

My brother and I both froze. If it was possible to become invisible, we did at that moment. Or tried. Maybe by some weird trick of Physics, or Optics, we might disappear right in front of everyone's eyes. Hidden in plain sight? Wasn't that an expression? Maybe it would happen to us?

My father stood up in the now silent hall, a wagon wheel chandelier hovering above him. He walked angrily toward me, and I swear he started to remove his belt. I'm convinced he was about to whip us both right then and there, Wild West style.

Everything stopped. The Golden Nugget froze in time. The only sound was that of my grandmother's voice, unstoppable, still mouthing to no one in particular how "Helen Johnson was a friend of Sue Lessinger's, we played bridge a few times but that was years ago and you know Helen was always rather svelte, emaciated, but really lovely in a way, quite lovely really, and she and her husband had a granddaughter that boarded a horse somewhere near Terre Haute, and I think won several blue ribbons and is now, the granddaughter, married to a man who evidently is quite high up at Berry Plastics, so . . ."

First Kiss

It was at one of those fairs. The 4-H Fair, near where we lived in southern Indiana. We could walk there if we wanted, but it would take an hour or more. My mom dropped us off. We were eleven or twelve, in middle school, not yet ashamed to be seen with our mother. My friend Bill Portman and I. I'm sure he's still alive. I don't know. I don't like looking people up on the internet. I've made that mistake before. It's better not to know. That's how I found out Jason was dead.

My mom gave us each ten dollars to ride rides and eat. It was Saturday afternoon. I liked the carnival games. And I was good at them. I could beat any game—ring toss, darts, basketball, ski ball—it didn't matter. My brother and I shared a bedroom, and the walls were covered with prizes from the fair, those little framed mirrors that said Michelob or Pabst. I thought they were fantastic. But then I outgrew them. They're probably in a box somewhere. I paid a fortune in carnival tickets for those mirrors.

Bill and I bought ride tickets. We rode the Tilt-a-Whirl and then the bumper cars. The tickets went fast. We decided we better eat before the money was gone. When we passed the roller coaster, we changed our minds. The roller coaster lasted a minute and a half. We were broke. He had a dime and two pennies in his pocket. I found a nickel on the ground.

We went to one of those fast-food trucks that has a little bit of everything. We stood in line even though the cheapest thing was three bucks. I'm not sure what we were thinking. We were just looking at the menu. People lined up behind us, so we started moving forward.

Bill recognized Jenny Lerner's older sister Debbie working in the truck. She kept coming out and grabbing paper plates and soiled napkins from the tables and taking them behind the truck to some huge plastic bins. She was enormous. By enormous, I guess I mean she was sixteen, a sophomore in high school. Much older than us. Much taller than us. She had enormous hair, blue eye shadow, lipstick, and jeans with sequins down the leg. She was otherworldly. She'd been through puberty. She had hips, and breasts. Everything about her was enormous. At least compared to my diminutive stature, my scrawny arms and knobby knees. Her face and hair and thighs and make-up. Even the perfume she wore billowed out in a huge, sour, chemical cloud that you could taste as well as smell.

"Come on," Bill said, and pulled me out of line.

We followed Debbie between the food trucks to the back where she pulled out a pack of cigarettes and lit one.

"What do you twits want?" she said when she saw us.

"Can you get us some food?" Bill said. He knew her. I didn't. The two of them lived on the same street, and their parents were in a softball league together. I'd never said a word to her. In fact, she kind of terrified me.

"What! Are you serious?"

"We lost our money and we're starving. My parents can pay you back tomorrow."

"Fuck off."

"Come on . . . just some curly fries or something."

She pulled on her cigarette, exhaled a cloud of smoke in our faces, then said, "wait here."

We waited. Debbie walked out between the trucks to where the tables were. I could see the top of the Ferris Wheel spinning slowly over some locust trees that shaded the food court.

"Here," she said, coming back with a half-full paper boat of chicken wings. She offered them. I noticed a couple of the wings had bites taken out of them.

Bill grabbed one and bit into it. I declined.

"What, you don't like chicken?"

"Umm," I said.

Bill looked at me, then back at Debbie. "Is there anything else?"

"Jeezus Christ," Debbie said, "what do you think this is?"

"Come on," said Bill, "my parents will pay you."

She looked at him and shook her head. Then looked at me in a weird way. I smiled, I think. "Hold on . . . but you guys fucking owe me." She disappeared between the food trucks again.

A rat ran out of some bushes near the bins, crawled up one of them, and dove in. We looked at each other.

"She's just grabbing food off the tables," I said. "Food other people didn't eat!"

Debbie came back with a boat of curly fries in one hand, and some empty cups in the other. "Here, are you happy now?"

We reached for the fries.

"Uh uh, not yet . . ." she pulled the boat away.

"What?"

"You owe me."

"We only have seventeen cents."

"Give it to me."

Bill held out his coins. I held out my nickel. She had the boat of fries in both hands.

"Put it in my pocket," she said, and turned and pushed out her hip.

Bill did as she said. Something was weird. I wasn't sure what, but something was suddenly very weird. I put my nickel in her pocket, and she smiled.

We stood there for a second, then Bill reached for the fries. Debbie pulled them back again.

"Not yet," she said.

"Jeezus, what!"

"You still owe me."

"We don't have any money, Debbie."

She looked at me. "You're quiet," she said, "don't you talk?"

I looked at Bill.

"Come on Debbie," Bill said, "stop fucking around."

"Don't talk to me like that," she snapped, "you don't want me to tell the owner that I caught you guys stealing fries back here, do you?"

I got very nervous then. Bill said, "No."

"Do you want these curly fries or not?"

"Of course we do, Debbie."

"Well then," she said, and put the fries down on the generator attached to the truck. She walked over to me and said, "Don't fucking move. And don't say a thing."

"Okay."

"I said don't fucking say a thing!" she said. "Open your mouth." She grabbed my face and bent forward to kiss me on the lips. She put her tongue in my mouth. Her lip gloss smeared over my face. It tasted like bubble gum flavored cough syrup.

I just stood there, tasting her. I'm not sure why.

"Debbie," Bill said, "what the fuck are you doing?"

"Shut up," she said to him, "or I'm telling your parents."

"Telling them what?"

"You stole those fries."

Bill looked at me. I didn't want the fries anymore.

"Go out front and make sure nobody comes back here."

"What?"

"Do it or I'm telling your parents."

Bill looked at me. "Debbie this is crazy," he said, but he left. He walked out front. He left me there with her.

Once he'd gone, she turned to me: "Your friend's a little prick." She grabbed my face again, then leaned forward. She closed her eyes very dramatically and kissed me again. The taste was different this time. This time it was like old gum and shampoo.

She pushed me back against one of the bins. Her hands started moving over me. My whole body swelled, a weird kind of static electricity happened between us, electrons seemed to be building up in places that had no release. My legs were useless and I nearly fell, so she pressed me harder against the garbage bin. She moaned, I think. Or I did. Something moaned. She had her eyes closed and I could see through her hair to the Ferris Wheel, the locust trees, and a contrail that was writing its way across the sky.

WHAT THE BODY THINKS

There were many times we went to the river. My friend Jason and I. This was in Indiana. Southern Indiana. After high school, all our friends left town, went off to college, but we went to the river. He and I. Several times a week. He had an apartment a few blocks away and we'd walk down there when it got dark. The river was better after dark.

We drank whiskey. We drank Southern Comfort. We called it whiskey, though I'm not sure it was. Even now I don't know. We drank it straight (like Janis Joplin), passing the bottle back and forth. "Oh Lord won't you buy me a night on the town. Prove that you love me, and buy the next round." We sang and drank and felt young. I mean we could *feel* what it felt like to be young. It was a buzz. We were high on being young. It's hard to explain, and anyways, I'm not sure we understood it at the time.

We were great friends. The best. The only ones who didn't go to college. The only ones who read Kafka, Huxley, Vonnegut, Blake, Nietzsche. We called it philosophy, though I'm not sure it was. Even now I don't know. We were obsessed, he and I. We talked and talked about the equality of extremes, about the danger of dichotomies, about the illusion of Time and the betrayal of conformist thinking. We stayed up all night, watching the barges move coal and timber, gravel and pulp, up and down the river. That hot and humid, southern Indiana air.

Philosophy is a marriage of two Greek words, *philein* and *sophia*, meaning "lover of wisdom." Lover of learning. We thought everything that searched or was searching possessed a degree of philosophy. All that was new to us, excited us. And we philosophized about it. That is one advantage of not knowing very much: just about everything is new and exciting. The irony (lost on us, lost on me at least) was that while my one hand searched for wisdom, my other one repeatedly ignored it.

There was a diner downtown. It was open all night. When the whiskey was gone, we'd walk there and order breakfast. Sometimes we still had a little left in the bottle, and we'd spike our coffee with it. We rolled our own cigarettes and smoked them, our fingers stained, our teeth were brown. Old men sat alone reading newspapers. We knew we'd never be as old as them.

We were still kids. Eighteen. Young forever. That river and that diner were the center of our universe. And so were *The Flowers of Evil*, *The Marriage of Heaven and Hell*, *Siddhartha* and *The Complete Poems of Arthur Rimbaud*.

We were naïve, of course. I don't deny it. But we knew things then I no longer know. Some things you can only know when you're young. And if you miss it, well . . . you can never get it back.

Of course, we were miserable, too. I was always somewhere between attempted suicides. Jason just thought I was wild, I guess, reckless. We never mentioned it in terms of depression. After all, we believed in transcendence, in eternity. We wandered through a dark, romantic landscape. When we found out Anne Sexton mixed herself a gin martini and sat with the car running in her garage, while Billie Holiday sang from a cassette tape, we were ecstatic, in love. We could hardly contain our excitement. Or that Shelley purposely sailed directly into the heart of a storm and drowned. Or that Hart Crane jumped off the back of a ship in the Gulf of Mexico, saying only "goodbye, everybody." His body was never found. We laughed, we sang, we shouted their poems at the night sky and raised the bottle in their honor.

We worshipped Dionysus, Orpheus, the Bacchanals.

All the while the river lazed by. All those stars shining. The same stars that had been shining on the first humans. On the painters of Lascaux. On the druids who built Stonehenge. On the Incas, the Aztecs, the Sumerians and Mesopotamians.

"We all come from Africa," Jason said one night. And told me about early human life, how there were several species of human. How ours was the only one to survive. How we lived for over four million years before we ever stepped foot out of Africa, to Asia. Another two million years there, before migrating to Europe. How we've only been in the Americas a fraction of that time. A few thousand years at most. Hardly any time at all. "We've been around for millions of years! And those stars have been there the whole time. Watching us."

We looked up at the stars. Confused. Mesmerized. As if they were a kind of portal to and from the past.

"Neanderthal!" we yelled out over the river.

"Can you hear me!" we howled up at the night sky. And we believed! We were sure someone might hear us, someone above some million years ago. Listening now. We were part of them, and they us. Siblings. My brother, my twin (*"mon frère, mon semblable"*). The modern world was nothing but delusion. Madness. We cursed technology and the industrial revolution. We were fiercely Blakean. We despised the Christian Church.

At some point when we were nineteen, he met someone. He met someone and then he left. He moved to Louisville, which was a hundred miles away but might as well have been a million. I went to the river a few times alone, but it wasn't the same. It wasn't the same once he left.

Then I met someone. And I left.

I never felt that way again, like I did then, beside the river, when I was eighteen. We were naïve, of course. But we knew things then we no longer know.

Before the Flood

My mother and I used to walk around in the summer, picking wild-flowers from the ditch alongside the roads near our house. This was when we lived in southern Indiana. It was, I guess, rural. There weren't farms, though. It wasn't, I guess, that rural. But it wasn't sub-urban either. Something in between. The sticks. My mother called it the sticks. Compared to Milwaukee it was like a kind of Walden. Not delightful like Walden. More like those Friday-the-13th movies, where a group of teenagers are trapped in a house in the woods, and they're slowly hunted by a shadowy figure in a hockey mask. I guess my sib-lings and I were those teenagers. Or maybe it was just me.

I'm not sure when this was. What year it was and how young I would've been. When my mother and I would go pick flowers together. After it rained, the ditches would fill with water and sometimes flood onto the roads. Then, a few days after that, they'd be full of flowers. My mother loved Queen Anne's Lace, and Bachelor Buttons. There were daisies, too. I don't remember anything else. We'd gather a huge sheaf of them, and put them on our kitchen table or take them to my grand-mother's. The memory is hard to believe. That southern Indiana was ever that lyric. That bucolic. I have to think the fact that it's gone has made it more lovely. Has made it lovely at all.

Maybe I was in high school. It sounds nice, almost like a dream. The bright, clear days when she was with me, when we were together (without caring that we were together). It's hard for me to imagine we did that then. I was so miserable. Maybe it was earlier. Maybe I was a kid still. Maybe there wasn't any shadowy figure in a hockey mask yet.

A Great Tandem, A Great Darkness

I have a photograph of Jason and me. We must be only seventeen or eighteen. I'm not sure who could've taken it. Probably Sarah, Jason's girlfriend at the time, and soon-to-be wife. First wife. Without the photograph I'm sure I wouldn't remember that night at all. In fact, I still don't remember it. It's a photograph of a moment I am clearly present in—there's photographic evidence—but it may as well be someone else, someone no longer alive.

We're sitting on a log by the river. Smoking. One of us is smoking. I think it's me (I don't have the picture in front of me. It's lost in a box somewhere. I'm trying to remember it even though I've looked at it a thousand times), but he was the smoker. I smoked for ten years. I had some success, but ultimately couldn't make it happen. It never felt right. I never felt like "a smoker." Whereas he smoked until the day he died. His parents smoked. His grandparents smoked. For him it was genetic.

Once I visited him in Louisville. We were in our twenties. I had dinner with him and his wife, his second wife. After a dish of vegan lasagna (he was vegan, not me) he and I went for a walk. Two blocks from his house he picked up a tin can that was upside down in an alley. He pulled a pack of cigarettes out from beneath it. We walked and talked, he smoked, he chain-smoked, and then went back to put the cigarettes under the can before we headed home.

"I'm pretty sure she knows I still smoke," he said, "but if I don't do it in front of her, she doesn't say anything."

"You're like Raskolnikov when he hides the old woman's purse under the rock."

"Maybe," he said sadly, "but that also makes me the dead woman."

"True," I said, though I wasn't sure what he meant.

In the photograph it's night. I'm facing away from the camera, into the darkness where the river is but can't be seen. Jason has a 35mm camera and he's taking a picture of something off to the side. Even though it's dark and he has no flash. We used to take pictures of the moon, but he's aiming the camera too low. Somewhere there's a box with hundreds of pictures of the moon. Probably in his parent's basement. Though I'm not sure if his parents are still alive. I've thought about trying to get in touch with them, but I'm not sure they'd appreciate it. Part of me thinks they blame me for his death. Part of me thinks they're right.

I'm pretty sure in the photograph there's also a bottle of whiskey. With whiskey I had great success, if short-lived. I never was so drunk as the nights we drank whiskey by the half-gallon. You'll recall we were eighteen, that is, reckless, that is (for me anyway), suicidal. I found the floor of various county jails several times in my teens and early twenties, and whiskey always had something to do with it. Nearly everything to do with it.

Eventually I realized I had to stop drinking. We were just too symbiotic, whiskey and I. Like fire and kerosene. Or maybe it was more like the way ants exploit aphids. I was the aphid that the whiskey kept alive, milking me to its own ends. What is the Connolly quote? "What grape to keep its place in the sun, taught our ancestors to make wine?"

I was an obeisant sycophant to whiskey. Jason also had that peculiar gene that allows one to collapse into absolute passiveness and self-destruction. We were a great tandem descending into a great blackness.

In the photograph we look innocent enough. Young. Healthy. Our white T-shirts glowing in the hidden photographer's flash. In the photograph, even though it's all there—whiskey, cigarettes, the river and the fathomless darkness around us—you'd never guess the next fifteen years would be so terrible.

I guess that's why I look at that picture so much. There's something about it I can't fully understand. Jason's dead now, and in the picture he looks like a ghost: the white T-shirt against the black background, immense and overwhelming. It's odd to see him so alive. So young. Everything still ahead of us. A whole series of decisions that would, eventually, lead to his death still unchosen. In that picture, you can see that he still has a chance, is still capable of finding a way out . . . but maybe it's the same with any picture of anyone. Maybe someday, when I'm dead, someone will see me in that picture, someone who doesn't know Jason at all. Someone will see me and think, "huh, too bad . . . he was so young."

A Rolling Stone Gathers No Cops

Jason and I were living in a kind of flophouse in Louisville, a hippy house. There were anywhere between ten and twenty people staying there on a given night. Most of these people were tripping on acid or mushrooms. All of us were high. Jason and I didn't really fit in with these folks. We preferred whiskey to weed and acid, and Townes van Zandt to The Grateful Dead. But we were kind of stuck there. I'm not sure why.

One night we just left. We drove to New Orleans. We lived in his car for a while, a Ford Escort. Then, when the car got towed, we moved to the street. It's easy to move to the street. You just walk out onto the street and stay there. You don't have to fill out any applications or provide references. You just go stand around somewhere, or walk around somewhere, and after a while you're living on the street.

If you want, you can work while you're on the street. You don't have to, but you can, if you want. I worked as a harmonica player in New Orleans. No one hired me. I just started playing and sometimes people would give me money. Not very much. A few dollars a day. It was enough for me. Eventually, I made enough money to buy a clarinet from one of the pawn shops outside the Quarter. Then I worked as a clarinet player.

With the clarinet I made about as much money as I did with the harmonica. I didn't really know how to play, but what I did play sounded good to me. And must've sounded good to other people, too, because they threw a few dollars into the case. Next to the case I had a sign that said, "spare a few dollars for clarinet lessons." I never made enough to take lessons. After I bought cigarettes and St. Ides, there wasn't much left. A few months after I bought the clarinet, someone stole it, so I went back to working as a harmonica player.

We had a crew of friends in New Orleans who felt the same way I did. They too were living on the street. We were all teenagers. We hung out together, drinking coffee for long hours in the all-night cafes. We busked together. Jason had a job as a guitar player. He could play any song any tourist requested, and we sang the lyrics when we knew them, and improvised when we didn't. We started a band. A horrible band that sounded fantastic. We pooled our money and had wild parties in Jackson Square. Everyone was invited. All the tourists stared. After the parties we slept in doorways, or on the riverbank, or in St. Claude Cemetery. It was easy to climb over the wall of the cemetery.

The cops didn't like us. Nobody really liked us, I guess. Sometimes tourists took our picture because they thought we were insane, exotic, or otherworldly . . . I don't know what they thought, actually. But for some reason they wanted to take our picture. We charged them a dollar but should've charged more. I'm sure there are several pictures of Jason and me in photo albums in people's closets scattered throughout the Midwest. "Here we are in New Orleans. There's Jenni eating a beignet at Café du Monde, there's the Algiers ferry, there's St. Louis Cathedral, and look here are those animal people with face tattoos and jewelry everywhere. Remember how one of them carried around a dead rat in a shoebox? . . . Weird."

Sometimes the cops arrested us, and took us to jail, which we all called OPP (Orleans Parish Prison). Mostly they just told us to move on, that we couldn't loiter, etc.

We did what they said. Sort of. We walked around the block and resumed our party somewhere else. The cops would show up at our new "gig" and tell us to move again. When they got sick of this game, and especially if there was a big festival coming up—Mardi Gras or JazzFest— they would arrest us and take us to Orleans Parish Prison.

OPP was not a nice place. It was a cold and violent place. But we all agreed the food there was better than the food at the homeless shelters. At the homeless shelters they served you a plate of rice and some undefinable gumbo-ish thing in the shape of a blood splat. We learned very quickly to avoid the soup kitchens and the cops.

All my friends hated the cops and would sometimes yell at them and flip them off. I didn't mind the cops. I felt bad for them. They had to deal with us and a whole lot of other shit that I wouldn't want to deal with. I also thought there was a lot of truth in the things they were saying:

"You can't stay here." "You have to leave." "You gotta move on." etc.

At the time I was reading Nietzsche, and I was obsessed with William Blake's *Marriage of Heaven and Hell*. Jason and I memorized the best lines from Blake's "Proverbs of Hell" section: "Drive your cart and your plow over the bones of the dead," "the road of excess leads to the palace of wisdom," "if the fool would persist in his folly he would become wise," that kind of stuff. When we took a swig off the bottle, we'd say "drown him in the river who loves water." (I only learned recently that it's "dip" him, not "drown" him.)

To me, the cops spoke in aphorisms, too. Just like Blake. And their aphorisms weren't much different than the great poets, Zen masters, and ancient prophets. They were inarguable—"You can't stay here"—and proved to be true. Look at me now: no longer there. They were right: we couldn't stay there. Couldn't stay young. Couldn't keep working as a harmonica player. We did have to move on.

Jason, too. He moved on. He drank himself to death. Day after day, year after year. While I somehow rescued myself from that life, he never stopped what we'd started. Living on the street. Wandering from New Orleans to Louisville, San Francisco, Seattle, Santa Fe, and several dozen towns and cities in between. Singing "Gin and Juice" and "St. James Infirmary," "Brokedown Palace" and "The Old Laughing Lady."

Jason's gone now. The cops were assholes, and brutal, but they spoke the truth. You just can't stay where you are. You have to move on.

Your Requests

I remember I was still young. Not a kid, but young. I think I was twenty-three or four. It was 1995 or 6. It was dark.

Not that being young was dark, or the '90s were dark—I mean they *were* dark, in a way, at least for me—but it was literally dark. It was three or so in the morning. I had an apartment in a small town in the Northwest. I was staying up all night, listening to the local radio station, the one at the college. I did that sometimes back then, in the '90s when I was young.

This was after I decided to try to get my life together. To stop doing drugs. To stop living on the street. Jason and I had been sort of taking care of each other for a few years. Taking care of each other while at the same time enabling each other's self-destruction. I couldn't see him anymore. He wasn't interested in (or capable of) quitting that life. We'd bounced from town to town in a kind of traveling circus of bacchanalian self-immolation. After a while I just got sick of it. I couldn't handle it anymore. I decided to go to Alaska to work on a fishing boat, to make some money that I could use to pay the tuition for my first year in college. I asked him if he wanted to come. We could do it together. We could lift ourselves out of the alleys and flophouses and doorways and grime. He declined, and that was basically the end for us. I left that world. He stayed in it. We never really saw things the same way again.

It was three or so in the morning and I had called into the station. On a landline. That's all there were then, landlines. I had a phone that was made to look like a mallard duck. Very realistic. It quacked when someone called, but the ringer was damaged, so instead of a quack it was kind of like a kazoo, a poorly played kazoo. It didn't take pictures. The very idea of taking a picture with a phone seemed absurd. Why would you even want to? I found the duck phone at a garage sale in Tacoma, Washington. It was very kitsch. I liked kitsch when I was young.

You could call and talk to the DJ back then, in the '90s. I wasn't doing anything, just listening to the radio. I waited until the DJ had finished talking and put on a song. Then I called. The DJ answered. I requested a song, and then the DJ asked what I was doing awake so late.

"Nothing. Just waiting out the night, I guess."

"Well, I'll try to get your song played in the next hour or so."

"Great."

". . . but we have a lot of requests tonight."

"Ah."

". . . but I think I can get to yours."

"That would be great."

"Okay, keep listening."

"I will."

"And thanks for calling in."

She hung up the phone, and not long after, the song on the radio ended. The DJ's voice came on to say something about the previous song, and then introduced the new one. The new song was not the one that I requested. I think I had a crush on the DJ. I had a crush on the DJ's voice. I had no idea what she looked like, but I loved her voice. There was something delicious about her voice, coming out of the radio, disrupting the immensity and silence, that darkness at the cul de sac of night. Her voice was a profound reprieve, a cry in the dark. I imagine that's what Narcissus heard when he heard Echo for the first time.

I'm not sure what I was doing sitting up all night. Just thinking, I guess, and listening to the radio. I did that sometimes back then. It was something you did in the '90s, just waiting out the night. Feeling the night as it grew dark, and that sense of profound isolation. How at some point it would shift and build toward dawn and all the things people would be doing that morning. I used to like to stay up for that. That long and baffling arc of emotion. That weird moment in time—a kind of termination zone—when everything changes, suddenly. From night to day. But specifically those moments right before morning that grow darker and darker, quieter, colder. I loved how much larger it was than me, how it has nothing to do with us, no concern or care, how it's beyond our control. I used to like to be awake for that. To feel it happen.

That's how it was in the '90s.

The DJ played several more songs and none of them were mine. I didn't really mind, though. It did make me wonder if she maybe didn't like my song. That would be sad. I tried not to think about it.

I was hoping she would play it before the mood shifted. It was a song that would only work in the desperate part of night. While it was still descending into bleakness. It was a terrible song for terrible lone-liness. If the DJ played it after the night had shifted, it wouldn't work. It would be all wrong.

I guess I should say that I wasn't lonely. I was just young. I was alone, sure. Okay maybe lonely, too, but I was enjoying it. I'd chosen it. Staying up all night was something to do. I knew it would be sad. But you're looking for that type of thing, that deep melancholy, when you're young. There's something comforting about it. And the song I requested, too, was like that.

The DJ came on again and I was happy to hear her voice. She said a few things about the song she'd just played, and then introduced the next one. It wasn't mine.

I'm not sure what I was doing. Thinking, I guess. I'm sure I was in some sort of relationship. But I was alone that night. I was proba-bly wondering if the relationship was serious or not. And I'm sure I figured it was not. I tried several times before I got it right. (Whoever said that the third time's the charm grossly underestimated the diffi-culty of finding the charm.)

I might've been thinking about work. Not that thinking is so com-partmentalized. Thinking tends to be promiscuous, it has poor bound-aries. For a while I worked in the library, but I also worked as a cook in a Chinese restaurant. Sometimes I did odd jobs for the landlord in ex-change for rent. I helped him put a new roof on the building one sum-mer. I didn't really have a plan. I didn't think of any career. I never really wanted that. Not when I was young. In fact, a career was the last thing I wanted.

What I wanted was to hear my song. It was getting late. Close to 4:30. Once it was 5:00 it would be too late. Night would be too pale, too optimistic. It would basically be morning, not night at all. There were other songs for that. My song wouldn't work as a morning song.

I thought about calling the DJ and telling her I didn't mind if she didn't play my song. It would be better than playing it when the sky was getting light, and people started waking up. That wasn't who the song was for.

The DJ came on the radio again and I knew she would play it this time. She'd said she knew the song, so she must've known it was a song for the darkest crevices of night. A song for the people at the bottom of the well. She said a few things about the songs she'd just played, and then she introduced the next one. It wasn't mine.

I'm not sure what I was doing. Thinking, I guess. I did that sometimes back then.

II.

These Are the Things
I Can Do Without

*In which the author becomes confused
by the behavior of his fellow
sentient beings*

What the Rain's Like

The rain here will beat you. You think it won't, but it will. I realize it's a cliché but, well, some clichés are clichés for a reason. In the Northwest, the rain is a cliché.

If it was just rain that would be one thing. It would still beat you, but maybe not as fast. It's the cold, too. The rain and the cold.

My first year in the Northwest I didn't notice it. I was twenty-one, and I worked in a bar. I washed dishes and worked my way up to line cook. I was a great chef of fish n' chips, burgers, omelets, and all things "short order." Grilled or fried or simply ladled from a pot. Our chili was to die for. It's possible a few people died from it.

My manager, in fact, had a heart attack and died while I was working there. Not from the chili, though. He was a recovering alcoholic who traded in his addiction to booze for a compulsive habit of Diet Pepsi and cigarettes. I never saw him without a pint glass of Diet Pepsi, ice, and a straw. He also smoked two packs a day. One day he didn't come into work and the owner said he was dead. Heart attack. If there was a funeral, I wasn't invited. He hadn't been there that long.

The next manager was a born-again Christian, and also a recovering alcoholic. He was a graduate from Cornell whose life was ruined by bad luck and cheap vodka. We worked the breakfast shift together, and he talked regretfully about his former life. I felt like I was in an AA meeting. I enjoyed working with him, listening to him tell me about his life while we flipped and folded hundreds of eggs Benedicts and Denver omelets . . .

But I digress.

The rain here will beat you. But not at first. I was twenty-one and working in a bar. After work each day, I stayed in the bar where I could drink for free. The owner was a cocaine addict, and he would give us coke sometimes when he had it to spare. He didn't like doing coke alone, so we'd go into the basement and snort lines and do shots of Jäger. I didn't like Jäger. But he was the owner, so I drank Jäger. He also owned a pistol. A revolver. I know it sounds crazy, but I remember passing it around, emptied of bullets, high on coke and daring each other to hold it against our heads and pull the trigger.

All of this is to say, I didn't really notice the rain that first year, when I was working in the bar, cooking breakfast in AA meetings every morning, drunk and on coke every night.

My second year was different. That winter lasted from mid-September to the end of June. The weather's different now, I know. It's hotter, and dryer. You might get warm days in May. But then, in the '90s, you never did. You couldn't escape it, the rain and the cold. It does something to you.

It's beautiful, of course, the way an Elliot Smith ballad is beautiful. A Rothko painting, or Chopin's nocturnes. Somber. Melancholy. The kind of beauty that makes you want to slit your wrists or jump off a bridge. Imbued with despair and mortality, opioids. Saturated with regret, darkness, nostalgia. Nostalgia for what? You don't know. A time before you ruined your life. The rain is like that. Not at first, but a week into it. A month into it. Every day the same nearly imperceptible variations on a repeating theme. And all those days accumulate, so that when it rains tomorrow, all the days of rain leading up to that day are evoked, and fall on your chest, fall into your darkest depths, as if all the ex-lovers who ever wronged you walk in at the same time, and sit at the bar, and stare at you, and want to talk through your issues with you, which plunges you further into absence, isolation, and hopeless dolor.

That's what the rain's like here.

●

CONNIVANCE

When my daughter was in seventh grade, she told me they watched a video about Hiroshima in her history class.

"It was so terrible, Papa. Their skin was peeling off, and the radiation turned people into zombies. The whole city was gone. All the people in it, and children who had nothing to do with the war. Papa, people melted or burned, and their eyes fell out. Even their bones were gone. Some people became ants. They called them ants. Their skin sort of just rotted on their bodies and they walked in straight lines, slowly. Papa, their brains were eaten by the radiation, and babies exploded or melted or just disappeared. Did you know about this, Papa? Did you know that happened?"

"Yes."

We were quiet then. I felt accused. And guilty. Was it me who dropped the bomb? Should I have told her about it? And the Holocaust? Have they studied that? Pol Pot? Dresden? The Salem Witch Trials? Does she know about R. Kelly? Should I tell her about Hugh Heffner and the Playboy Mansion? The Branch Davidians? Jefferey Epstein? Jeffrey Dahmer? Jeffrey Goldblum in *The Fly*? Am I the bearer of human atrocities? Is this what I've passed down? What mad and incomprehensible inheritance have I given her?

I was walking her home from school. I was carrying her clarinet. The day was cold and cloudy but then there was a little break, the sun fell through the sky and it was as if the air had flowered. Every aerosol filled with light, and the leaves and cars and street signs all seemed so brilliant, so fine and so lovely.

And then the clouds closed over again, and the air dulled again, dampened and grew cold again.

"Papa, it was so terrible."

On Writing Letters

I wrote a letter to Jason. It wasn't easy. He'd written me twice, and then called to say I should write him. That we should write letters again, like we used to.

We did used to. He was my best friend, I'd known him the longest, but we never lived in the same town for long. We'd known each other twenty years before I found out he died. Over that time, we saw surprisingly little of each other.

At first it was because I was trying to get my life together. To stop drinking. To stop doing drugs. I was sick of living on the street. I got a job as a dishwasher in a bar. I fell in love with one of the waitresses there. She was much smarter than I was. I thought I'd better go to college. I'd better start listening, and learning.

Jason couldn't shake the booze. Or didn't want to. I don't really know. It's confusing. Why one person is able to change their life, and the other dies.

I got married in my twenties. Not to the woman who was smarter than me. That didn't last long, but that relationship helped me get on the right path. A healthier path. My wife and I had a child. My wife and I got divorced. I was busy. Life was happening to me. Life was humbling me.

Jason and I mostly lost track of each other. After that period in New Orleans, as teenagers, taking care of each other on the streets, we never lived in the same town again. He was still drifting. He sent me letters from New Orleans, Santa Fe, San Francisco. I sent mine to his parents' house in Louisville. Sometimes I wasn't sure he ever received them. I just wrote them, and sent them, as if into the darkness. Sometimes I wondered if I should just bury the letters in a hole in the woods.

But he kept writing. And I kept getting his letters. Sometimes I could tell he'd received mine. Not always, but sometimes. For ten or more years we wrote letters to each other, wonderful letters. This was before the internet and email, before everyone carried a phone around with them. Before texting, and Zoom, and all the things that are good for business maybe, but not necessarily for friendships.

Then the letters stopped and honestly, I sort of forgot about him. I hate to say it, but it's true. I just had too much going on. Then, after not hearing from him for several years, there was a letter again. From Jason. In fact, he'd written me two letters in the span of a couple weeks. I was surprised, I guess. I'm not sure why I hadn't written him back yet. I owed him one. I hadn't written a letter to anyone in years. Ten maybe. I mean pen on paper, in cursive. I'm not talking about emails, that's different. That's easy. A letter is much more difficult than that.

I should point out that I write every day. I write with a pen on paper, in cursive every day. But that's mostly poetry, diary entries, little sketches, impressions of this weird world. I write every day, but it's not the same thing as writing a letter. A letter requires something unique. A sustained focus. A certain sincerity. A certain chemistry. A letter is like a grandfather clock. It's like a steam train, an iron, a walk. A letter is from a previous century. You have to slow down, but the slowness is hard. It nearly breaks you. A letter is constantly in danger of breaking down, of coming apart at the seams.

I suppose it's because our thoughts come too quickly now. We've been conditioned to be scatter-brained. To follow a single thought over two handwritten pages is a near-impossible task. There's a constant temptation to let other things in. You'll have a thousand thoughts in any five-minute slab of consciousness. And it takes much more than five minutes to write a two-page letter.

My letter was four pages. It took me three separate sessions to write it. I had to be in the mood. I went to the park once, with a thermos of coffee. It was October. The sun was out, and the leaves were just beginning to fall. But still, I could only get a page-and-a-half written. I spent two hours there. Two hours and then I couldn't go on any longer. By the time the second hour was up, I was exhausted.

The next session was a few days later, late morning on a moody, rainy day. I played records and wrote. Bill Evans, I think, or that Mingus album where he plays solo piano. I could only write for three sides—a record and a half—before I had nothing interesting to say. Or rather, before I realized I wasn't saying anything interesting.

For the third session I went out and sat on the front steps of the art school near my place. The sun was back. And the leaves. I wrote for about an hour before a security guard asked if I was a student there.

I wasn't.

"Professor?"

"No."

He said I had to leave.

I said I was just trying to finish a letter to my friend.

He said he was sorry, but I had to leave.

I told him my friend had already sent me two letters and I was worried he was going to send me a third before I replied to his first one.

The security guard said he didn't care. He asked why I didn't just send him an email. "Or call him for gods sakes."

"It's not the same," I said.

He said I had to leave. Again.

I left. I went back to the apartment and found an envelope, a stamp. I quickly finished the letter: ". . . wishing you the absolute best . . ."

I walked three blocks to the mailbox. When the blue door slammed shut, I felt a great relief. The letter was done. I could go back to writing things that weren't letters again.

When I got home, Liz said there was mail for me on the kitchen counter: some bills, a magazine, and something from Jason.

Sex and Food, I Guess

Liz and I drove up to one of those little towns on the Sound. One of those little towns where the sea gulls start laughing at 5 a.m. and don't stop until midnight. I'm not sure how they do it, or what is so worth babbling on about. Sex and food, I guess.

The tourists, by contrast, don't do much laughing at all. Oh sure there is the occasional sigh, a smile, an oh-how-lovely remark while staring out at the mountains reflecting in a calm September sea, but any laughter seems forced. I'm not sure why. Perhaps they sense they're getting fleeced. The clams and calamari are a wee bit over-priced, a tad too undercooked.

Unlike the sea gulls, the tourists are all food, no sex, and have the fried cheese curd physiques to prove it. Did they sail here in their RVs just to buy saltwater taffy and fudge? To order artichoke dip and Aperol spritz? Or to sip a chardonnay from a "local winery" 300 miles away?

Liz and I had a great time in our reassembled Victorian kitsch hotel, listening to the laughing gulls, the rigging on the masts in the marina, and the leaf blower at 7 a.m. (I'm pretty sure there weren't any leaves on the ground, and if there were they could've been picked up, in silence, in little more than a half-hour with a broom and dustbin.)

One night we went to the Lilac Theatre, a "vintage" theatre from the 1930s. One hundred years is ancient in the Northwest. The Lilac is truly beautiful. Truly baroque in relation to these undecorated times. It was a pleasure just to sit in the red velvet chairs, to stare up at the ceiling, wild with mischievous cherubs and various displays of cornucopia.

We showed up for the movie forty-five minutes early (not having much else to do in such a town) to eat popcorn and admire the sconces. In fact, that's why we went to the Lilac, to watch the theatre itself, rather than the movie. We sat and chatted and wondered at the ornate ceiling as if we were in the Sistine Chapel. We had the place mostly to ourselves. A few old men were scattered about, each by himself, patiently waiting for the action to start. The lonely movie-goer is a sad and endangered bird. I worry they will soon be extinct.

The previews eventually came on, and we enjoyed them, but when the movie began—some sort of Hollywood disaster that was essentially a continuous series of car chases and explosions wrapped around the most unbelievable (and least sexy) sexual tension between two mostly AI-generated characters who would never be together in real life—when the previews were over and the movie began, we left.

Outside, the air was fragrant with the rich pheromones of a saltwater bay at low tide. Every clam shell and oyster open to the air and effervesced. The piers were empty silhouettes. The night sky looked down with a dim smattering of stars. Sea gulls silent at last. The sound of the rigging rang in the marina, making the night air seem colder than perhaps it was. Not a single tourist waddled web-footed down the dark seaside streets. All of them, evidently, returned to their rooms, quietly bloated, silently flatulent, lowered down into their highly pillowed memory foam beds.

These Are the Things I Can Do Without

They put a bank where the gay bar was. Where the gay bar had been for thirty years. I'd say that pretty much sums it up. What's happened to the neighborhood. To the city, really. It was a dive bar. Everybody went there.

It was a fantastic place. By which I mean to say it was a dump. A dark and filthy hole. Fantastic. They had food but you wouldn't want to eat it. You didn't go there for the food. You went there for the cheap drinks or to hook up, or both. We went there for the drinks, and the jukebox.

They still had an old-school jukebox, and you could play just about any song you could think of, as long as it was gay. There were only gay songs on the jukebox. Five songs for a dollar, which when you're drunk enough, seems like a great deal. This was years ago. They had Madonna, Cher, Barbra Streisand, Chris Isaak, George Michael, Culture Club, Village People, etc. All the classic hits. We mostly played Queen or Morrisey.

One night with Jordan—who was going through a break-up—we played all the Chet Baker songs they had. I think it cost us ten bucks, a double album. There were some drunk queens in drag who weren't pleased with our selection: "Oh honey this man is so depressing," they yelled at the beginning of each song. "Play some Diana Ross will you, puh leeze!"

But we'd already pressed the buttons, there was nothing to be done. The queens complained for an hour and more about how you can't dance to "this jazz shit or whatever it is. Honey what *is* this!"

After "My Funny Valentine" one of them yelled at the bartender, "Sweetie bring me another drink . . . and a lethal dose of Prozac." The whole bar laughed, and we all were cured, for a moment or two, of our broken hearts.

But that's all done. There's a bank there now and nobody plays music or gives hand jobs in the booth near the bathroom while Tears for Fears sings "Shout. Shout. Let it all out . . ."

When the bank opened, they put a pride flag in the window for a few months, as a sort of gesture of respect I guess, but they eventually took it down. Sometimes when I walk by there I can still hear the music, "You shouldn't have to sell your soul."

DON'T TELL ME YOUR DREAMS

My friend knows everything about his dreams. That is, he knows what they mean, and he'll go on and on about what he dreamt about and what it symbolizes.

I don't mind having dreams, but I don't like talking about them. And I absolutely abhor anything resembling dream interpretation. I'm glad I didn't live in the mid-20th century. All that Freudian, Jungian psychoanalytic pseudoscience . . . horrible. Even when my wife—whom I love—starts to tell me about her dreams, I immediately feel claustrophobic. It ruins the morning for me. I leave the room. I leave because if I don't leave, I get irritable. I know myself. I despise talking about dreams.

Sometimes she—my wife (whom I love)—tells me about her dreams before I have a chance to get out of bed. First thing in the morning. I'm not even really awake yet. As consciousness dawns on me, I realize she's talking about her dreams. I'm trapped. By the time she's done describing them, I can't hide my distaste.

"What's wrong?"

"I've told you before," I say, apologetically, "I can't stand talking about dreams."

"Why not?"

"I don't know."

"Well what did you dream about last night?"

"Nothing."

I always say nothing, even if I've had the most wonderful dream. I don't want anyone to tell me what my wonderful dream *means*. I don't want anyone even knowing what I dream—even my wife (whom I love). My dreams are my dreams. In a world where there's less and less privacy, dreams are about the only place where no one can see you. No phone is listening. No one's overhearing. No data's being gathered. And no one's commenting.

I like to think of dreams as if they are a snowfall on a warm, forty-degree day: they just appear, flurry about, then melt away. That's a perfect dream interpretation, one that doesn't interpret at all. There's no need to ask, "what did it mean when the flakes blew this way, that, when they swirled up into the streetlight, or fell fast and heavy onto the driveway?" Who cares? Were they beautiful? Yes. Terrible? Yes. Did you slip on the ice? Yes. That's it. Leave them alone.

To parade your dreams around on a regular basis, and ostentatiously propound on the (always profound) meaning of them shows, I think, an incredible amount of narcissism. We live in an overly revealing society. Why does everyone think their experience is so interesting? The exhibitionism long ago reached shameful proportions. It's something like a nudist on the beach . . . it may feel good to you to be naked but that doesn't mean other people want to see it. Why do you need to reveal yourself to enjoy being alive? Show some discretion. Some taste. Grab a towel for gods sakes!

With respect, my dreams are my dreams, and yours are yours. I'd like to keep it that way if you don't mind.

LET ME TELL YOU A DREAM

My father's parents owned a timeshare in Fort Meyer's Beach when we were kids. My brother and I played tennis there. They had a small condo in a huge building. They didn't have it very long, but I remember going there a few times. In spring, I guess. Or maybe summer. We drove down from Milwaukee in a brown station wagon. People didn't fly as much, then. If you had a station wagon, you took that.

I had nightmares when I was a kid. I still have nightmares. I never tried to figure out why. My mom says she has nightmares, too. I guess I got them from her, if you believe in that type of thing—the passing down of nightmares from one generation to the next. I suppose that's one way of looking at the history of humankind.

In one of the dreams recently, someone was tearing my dictionary apart. I couldn't tell if he was doing it intentionally. He was just letting it fall apart. And it did fall apart. It was falling apart. I watched, helpless. It doesn't sound like much, but I assure you it was terrifying.

My brother and I weren't very good at tennis, but we had energy. Endless energy. What we lacked in skill, we made up for in spite, in determination, and a competitive hatred only known to brothers. We may have been from a family whose grandparents owned a timeshare with tennis courts, but we were not from a family who took tennis lessons. We were self-taught. We willed the ball over the net. Often we just hit it as hard as we could, hoping it might hit our opponent in the face. We would take turns being John McEnroe and Björn Borg. My brother was blond and actually looked like Björn Borg. I had the mouth of McEnroe. The tennis matches usually ended in a fight.

At one point in the dream, a former neighbor of mine who'd been kicked out of his apartment tried to run me over with his motorcycle. He blamed me for kicking him out, which was somewhat fair since (1) I manage the building where he lived, and (2) I was the one who posted the eviction notice on his door. The dictionary was now in shreds. I was able to avoid my former neighbor for most of the night, but eventually he succeeded. Eventually he just ran right over me. Nothing ever hurts in my dreams. Things just happen.

My grandparents were of the country club age. Born in the twenties. They were in their twenties during World War II. Perhaps the country club age was a coping mechanism for the horrors of the atomic age, the mass-killings of the war, and the tense, uncertain future of the Cold War on the horizon. The country club as antidote for existential crisis.

My grandparents golfed and bowled and played bridge and pinochle right through Vietnam. My father got married, had all four of his kids before the war in Vietnam was over. His draft dodger's capital was high. He was white, married, had four kids, and a sports hernia. He wasn't drafted. I suppose he could've volunteered, but maybe the hernia would've kept him out?

The dream lasted all night. It's difficult to describe. Dreams are like action movies to me. They don't make any sense. They're just a series of fights, murders, and screaming. And there's never enough sex.

It was 1980-something. The early '80s. When we were in Florida playing tennis. I was ten or less. My brother is two years younger. My sisters are three and seven years older than me. They were never around. Sometimes I think about that. About how I never knew where my sisters were. At least until I went through puberty. Then I always knew. That is, if one of their friends was over, I always knew. Then I just hung around them, or tried to, with no idea what to do or say. I wasn't sure why I was even hanging around.

After he ran me over—the neighbor whom I'd arguably kicked out of his apartment—he grabbed an iron poker. In my dream the iron poker was called an andiron. I remember that very clearly, the word andiron. Even though it wasn't an andiron, it was an iron poker. Anyway, the former neighbor of mine grabbed the iron poker and crushed my skull with it. He kept crushing and crushing my skull. I watched from a tree branch nearby. It went on long after I was dead. Most of the times when I get murdered in my dreams, the murder continues happening long after I'm dead.

They would take us to play miniature golf. For a long time I thought miniature golf only existed in Florida. As the orange blossom is Florida's state flower, I assumed miniature golf was the state sport. We said "miniture" golf. Three syllables, not four. I liked miniture golf, but even as an adolescent I found some of the holes a bit overthought. Overwritten. They were just trying too hard to be witty, those holes. It wasn't curiosity that killed the cat. Overthinking, overdesign, killed the cat.

When I came down from the tree, I walked past my former neighbor, who was still engaged in my destruction, still thrashing me with the poker. (The poker, I might note, was *not* red hot. It wasn't hot at all, though it was red from all the blood everywhere. I realized this in the dream—the fact that the red poker was not a red-hot poker—but only as a trivial piece of information, a sort of subtext.) I walked past him and down the stairs to the subway. In the subway there was a kid, something like my tennis-playing self, who began antagonizing me. I told him to leave me alone, but he wouldn't. He kept saying, "You want me to cut you? You want me to cut you, don't you?" "No," I said, and I called 9-1-1. The dispatch put me on hold. While I was on hold the kid reached around my back and cut me. He cut me badly. My skin and muscle splayed open easily, like a fish. In the dream I even smelled fish. My open body smelled like fish.

I tried to hold the kid off with my free hand while holding my phone with the other. He reached around again, and sliced me open again. Blood was spraying everywhere, and I was furious with 9-1-1. I decided to give up, I hung up. The phone wouldn't fit in my pocket, though, and while I was trying to shove it in, the kid sliced me open again.

I still liked playing miniture golf, even though the holes were overdesigned. My brother and I would hit the ball and see if we could "accidentally" get it to roll all the way out into the street. My grandfather found this unamusing. The last hole on the course, the one that steals your golf ball and somehow (pneumatically?) returns the ball to the office, always made me sad. Each time we played I would experience a tremendous sense of loss when we reached the last hole. A kind of grief, I guess. And also a profound sense of being duped. For this reason, I always feel tricked when someone close to me dies. When I think of divinity personified (which I almost never do, but when I do), I always think of a Jester. The fact that Jason's dead is profoundly sad to me, but part of me doesn't trust that it's true. Part of me feels like he's still alive somewhere, and I'm the butt of a cruel joke.

A train came then. We were in the subway. It was an express. It didn't stop. Faces in the windows sped by me. I thought they would see me and try to call 9-1-1, but the faces just stared, bored, while the kid cut me again and again and I tried in vain to put the phone in my pocket. I had been dead for a long time, but the kid kept carving me. It was the second time I died that night.

Tennis was popular in the '80s, mostly because of Andre Agassi. He was young and cool and everyone loved his hair. His hair was the same as John Stamos' hair, but blond. My sisters had a huge crush on him. On both of them. I tried to grow my hair out but it didn't look very good.

Then I was suddenly *on* the train. The train was delayed and we were just sitting there. I could see me on the platform. I was already murdered but the kid kept cutting me. He had scissors now like those pizza scissors they give you at Neapolitan-style pizzerias. I looked out at me already murdered, a pool of wet meat on the platform floor, and the kid on his knees working at me. Cutting me into bits and then sewing parts of me to other parts. I don't know where he got the needle and thread.

I miss my grandparents. I loved the way they drank martinis, and moved slowly across the room with the martini glasses in their hands. They had a Cadillac with leather seats and sometimes I can smell it. And sometimes when I smell a tennis ball I think of them, too. And the miniture golf plastic grass. When I see fake grass, I think of them. And how hot it used to get on the tennis court in Florida.

When the train went into the tunnel, I suddenly saw my reflection. I don't know why but that was the most terrifying part of the dream, my reflection. I went from watching me being cut up and sewn back together, to seeing my face staring back at me. When I saw myself so close, I gasped and woke up.

A Hairdressers Tale

It rained today. September 12. I will remember the date, so extraordinary. After an entire summer of drought and forest fires, it finally rained. A mist really. A sort of drizz. Something a lot like but a little less than a full-on drizzle. Just a drizz. Of course, a drizzle isn't much either. A drizz is less than that. Nebulous. But still, it was a welcome sight to see, the drizz, bead on the akebia leaves, then roll down and fall to the ground.

We went for a walk in it. The drizz. There's nothing better. A walk in the rain after three months of dry summer air. That air finally cleaned of its dust and smog. The breezes bringing drops down. Mist swirling in the sky.

My grandmother found the drizz a nuisance. My father's mother. Once, not long before she died and sometime after my grandfather had, she flew out to visit. This was twenty years ago or more. I had decided to go back to college. I was living here then, too, in the Northwest. She seemed humbled by old age and her husband's death. She was close to eighty. She was lonely, I guess. She wanted to come out to see me. Or maybe she wanted to travel one last time. We weren't really that close, but we had a good time. That trip was the last time I saw her.

The day after she arrived, we drove to the Oregon Coast, where the drizz was doing its thing. Not necessarily falling, but whirling around in a mad dance of indirection. My grandma didn't like it. She wore a huge raincoat that only took on water and then ushered the drops down to her pants, which in the short walk from the car to Sea Lion Caves became soaking wet.

But that's not what really irked my grandma. Not her wet pants. It was her hair. She'd recently gotten her hair done. That's how she always said it. "I have to get my hair done." I liked the way she said that. No matter that I couldn't really tell the difference between undone and done, except that when it was done it looked a bit more ridiculous.

Of course, I wouldn't tell her that her hair looked ridiculous. You wouldn't say such a thing to your grandmother. Instead, when she says, returning from the salon: "oh well now at least my hair is done and we can go out in public again . . ." you say, "yes indeed," and "aren't you looking fine!"

At the Sea Lion Caves she wore one of those clear plastic rain hats that old ladies seem to always have. Where do they get them? They must all shop through the same catalogue. She was wearing it (I didn't even see her put it on; it was just suddenly covering her head, her hair). The clear plastic rain cap wasn't effective. It was no match for the multi-directional perseverance of the drizz. Her hair was soon undone. Before we even got from the parking lot to the entrance of the Caves, she said, "I can see that I'll have to find a place to get my hair done later today."

We took an elevator down to the cave. The stench was overwhelming. Not in the elevator, but in the cave. My grandmother looked visibly shocked. She tried to speak, to say something about the sea lions, but couldn't seem to open her mouth. We watched them dive off the rocks, and lug their huge bodies around, flapping their flippers and grunting, or belching, or barking. It was exhausting just to look at. I could tell my grandma was upset, uncomfortable, miserable. There was nowhere to sit that wasn't soaked. Somehow the drizz had made its way into the cave. The grunts were obscene, and the smell so horrid it seemed like it might solidify, turn to feces in mid-air, and then just drop like a turd. It was a cold dark ring in Dante's hell, and I had brought my grandmother there.

Later, in the car, when she took the clear plastic rain cap off, her hair deflated like a popped balloon. She immediately flipped the sun visor down to look in the mirror. "Oh my," she said, her suspicions confirmed, "we will have to find a place to get my hair done."

We were pretty far from even the smallest town. I suggested it might be difficult to find a place to get her hair done. Perhaps it could wait until Portland?

She pulled the visor down again, and looked in the mirror. "I don't think so."

I loved my grandmother. We weren't very close, but so what. She was my grandmother. That said, I didn't think her flat hair was cause for alarm.

I was wrong: "Your grandfather always seemed to find what I needed."

"Yes," I said.

"He was a very good man."

"Yes, I know. He taught me how to bowl," I said, not really knowing what to say.

She was with my grandfather the night he died. They had a room they called "the den." The TV was in that room, and an exercise bike, and two easy chairs with striped upholstery. They were watching the news and drinking martinis (as a child I heard her order a "dry martini on the rocks with a twist" at least a hundred times). My grandfather stood up to mix a second round, took a couple steps, then screamed and dropped dead. It wasn't a scream, I guess. My grandmother later said it sounded like an animal being slaughtered, like his soul had suddenly rushed out of him at once. His heart and lungs burst, exploded. She watched it all happen. She heard it all happen. She knew he was dead. She called 9-1-1, but she knew he was dead. One moment he was there, drinking with her, and then the next he wasn't. Seventy years gone in an instant, collapsed on a cream-colored shag carpet. His head hit the exercise bike that's now in my parents' basement. My mother said she hangs laundry on it sometimes.

She was trying to fluff up her hair in the mirror, but it wasn't working. "I'm afraid we'll just have to find a hairdressers."

"A hairdressers?"

"Yes, a hairdressers." That's how she said it, "a hairdressers." Plural. Or maybe it's possessive, as in "a hairdresser's shop." I'm not sure.

"Grandma, we're in the middle of nowhere. I'm not sure we can find one . . ."

"I miss your grandfather terribly."

"Yes," I said, "I do too."

"He was a very good man."

"We can stop in the next town, if you want? I don't know if they'll have what you're looking for, but we can see."

"That would be nice." She closed the mirror and flipped the visor back up.

We drove north up the coast. There were various points of interest, vistas, historical markers, etc. places to look out over the sea for whales, porpoises, pelicans, seals. Beautiful places. Sublime places. But we drove past them all, urgently in need of a hairdressers, which we eventually found, in Waldport, Oregon. Population: 2033. Hairdressers: 1.

NARCISSUS IN BEIJING

> "Curiosity is only vanity. We usually only want to know something so that we can talk about it; in other words, we would never travel by sea if it meant never talking about it."
>
> —Pascal, *Pensées*

My friend went to China. He's on a writing residency there. Or rather, he's on Twitter, Instagram, Tiktok and Facebook there. I'm not sure if he's writing. He says on Twitter that he is, but people lie all the time on Twitter. That seems to be what it's for. I think they call it, "personal branding."

I hope he's writing. I hope he's able to stop posting pictures of himself. It must be difficult for him to actually be in China if he's always checking his phone to see who, back in the U.S., "liked" the picture of him in China.

If he is writing, I don't imagine China will have much to do with it. It will mostly be about himself, or how he had a hard time engaging the culture. It will be a "personal essay," which is to say, a kind of literary selfie. Or else he'll lie and say Chinese culture is so welcoming and easy to engage. But anyone can see from his social media posts that he's more interested in *himself in China* than he is in *China itself*.

Maybe I should show some compassion for my friend. Maybe it's not his fault. Maybe it's a "condition of modern society" that we've lost our ability to get lost. To lose ourselves in the environment outside ourselves. It's troubling to me, this inability to step away from the mirror, from our self-constructed brand. Imagine Narcissus, standing on a corner in Beijing, staring down at his reflection. The city unseen all around him. Beijing! Thousands of years old, full of millions of people, restaurants, museums, galleries, taxis, temples, parks and gardens . . . and yet Narcissus holds his camera out only to point it back at himself, a few red lanterns glowing in the background as he purses his lips, turns his head to get the best angle, then snaps the selfie and pushes "post."

A good picture, to be sure, but I'd respect him more if I never saw him again.

Edvard Munch and the Electric Leaf Blower Massacre

"Was it Munch?" she was saying, "or was it one of the Bauhaus painters? Or was Munch one of the Bauhaus painters, too? I can't remember. Oh damn I hate this whole not remembering thing . . ."

"I don't know what Munch or Bauhaus has to do with it," I said, "the man didn't mention them. You're the one who brought them up. He was talking about leaf blowers and lithium batteries. How he'd heard that lithium is just as bad or worse for the environment than gas, than oil. And some electric leaf blowers are just as loud as gas-powered leaf blowers. Munch has nothing to do with it . . ."

"Wasn't he Norwegian?"

"Who? The guy with the leaf blower?"

"No. Munch. He wasn't German I don't think."

"I don't know. I thought he was Swedish maybe."

"His name is Edvard."

"Edvard?"

"Edvard. That's not Norwegian, Edvard."

"I wouldn't know."

"I wouldn't either, but he wouldn't be Bauhaus if he was Norwegian . . . or would he?"

"How should I know? And what's that got to do with lithium? Or the guy with the leaf blower?"

"I really think modern architecture is one of the worst things to happen to human civilization."

"Wow. Okay . . ." I said. She often did this kind of thing. Introduced, as a non sequitur, some sort of provocation.

"One of the worst things to afflict humankind."

"Uh huh. And not, say, I don't know, the plague? Genocide? Industrial pollution? Mass incarceration?"

". . . but modern architecture and the way it's been imposed on us *is* a kind of mass incarceration!"

"Uh huh . . ."

"Of course. It's an imposition on the psyche."

"Well, what isn't an imposition on the psyche? If architecture is, then everything is. Mass media, corporate greed, Dostoevsky, bowling alleys, homeless people selling flowers on the street . . ."

"You know what I mean."

"No, not really. I was talking about the guy I ran into. The landscaper who was using an electric leaf blower, and you started talking about Munch. Munch wasn't an architect; he was a painter. Unless . . . wait, is he the one who designed a house for his sister?"

"Think of the way our eyes transmit things to our brain . . ."

"Maybe that was Wittgenstein . . . I think that was Wittgenstein."

"From a cognitive science perspective, don't you think the things we see have a direct and powerful impact on how we see ourselves? On how we feel? On our mental health?"

"You're incorrigible," I said, though I wasn't sure that was the right word. I'd heard someone use it recently to great effect, so I thought I'd try it.

"Think about it. When you walk into a room, a space, any space, how that room is arranged has a direct correlation on how you feel. A warm yellow or red will produce one emotion, while a cool blue or green will produce another. A tiny apartment shapes a psyche much differently than an expansive villa."

"Uh huh." I think it was my mother in-law, actually, who used the word.

"And when you leave the city, you get out of your car and suddenly you're at the lakeshore . . ."

"The lakeshore?"

"The lakeshore . . . all that vast expanse around you. Stretching out in front of you . . ."

"Uh huh." By my mother in-law I mean, of course, *her* mother. Her mother has an immense vocabulary. Once, ordering a coffee at a café near our house, I heard her use the words inveigle and jejune in a single sentence, as if it were the most natural thing to do. The barista seemed a bit confused, but got her order right nonetheless.

"Stretching out to the horizon."

"Sounds lovely," I said.

"It *is* lovely. That's exactly the point! You're not in a room, you're at the lakeshore. The horizon stretching out, or rather the lake stretching out, and the sky stretching out, too. And not only is it lovely, but that loveliness produces a relaxed feeling in your brain. Inside/outside. The world outside effects the world within. I'm not crazy."

"Are we done with the leaf blower then?"

"One thing that does bother me, though, is that no one thinks of the sky stretching out. We always refer to the lower plane: lake, sea, field, road. That's the one, the lower one, that's stretching out to the horizon."

"Done with the lithium batteries? If so, fine, but I just don't know what's true anymore . . ."

"Never the upper, the sky, the sky is also stretching out to the horizon. What's the Zen quote? 'one hair between them . . . earth sky.' Is that it? No one ever mentions that."

"Are we really in an age of post-truth? A post-factual age?"

"I think we think somehow that the sky *is* the horizon."

"The guy was saying lithium batteries are worse than gas. Is that true? Or is that just some bullshit propaganda from the oil industry?"

"As if the lake stretches out, hits the horizon, and the sky stretches back towards us. It's a misnomer, I guess."

"What's weird, though, is he was using a lithium-battery-powered leaf blower."

"A name unsuitably applied."

"I know what a misnomer is . . . a lot of people are saying they're worse than gas now. Is that true? Or reactionary?"

"And too it's something like a dead metaphor I think."

"I'd like to see the data, personally. People shouldn't just go spouting their opinions unless they have a primary source. Maybe we should start demanding citations in conversations. Footnotes. Reveal your sources, please!"

"It's just kind of caught on, become a sort of meme, I guess. An accepted way of seeing."

"Exactly, there should be data. People shouldn't just question *everything.*"

"No."

"Or accept everything."

"No."

"Not without data. The proper data. Real facts!"

"Strata, that's it. We emphasize the lower strata, or stratum, in the bifurcation the horizon produces."

"Data. Not strata . . ."

"I know, it just reminded me of strata . . . that's the right way to think of it."

"It would be better if we could agree on something . . . anything."

"I agree. Even something as simple as what's up and what's down. Even that would be a great help."

"Agreed, anything at all. You can't just question everything. There has to be some solid ground."

"Language is flawed."

"Sure, but so is the mind. The mind is far more flawed than language. Language is just the material we use to communicate. The mind is the brush, and the hand, what we wield. It's no use arguing without the foundation of agreed-upon truths. If two minds can't agree on a single set of facts, no perfect language can possibly help."

"No, I guess not."

"That used to be the role of trusted institutions."

". . . designed in a neo-classical style to instill authority, certainty, Truth."

"But now all we want to do is tear down these institutions. Iconoclasm has become the rule. What's actually a great accomplishment, though, is the formation of institutions in the first place. I mean think of it. We were monkeys once! And then, suddenly, Temples, Pyramids, the Tower of Jericho, the Parthenon, the Roman Forum, colosseums!"

"I don't think 'suddenly' is the right word, but I see your point."

"My point is that anyone can smash an icon. But the establishment of icons takes time, and a sustained collective effort. A real feat of human cooperation, innovation, and industry. There's no use just willynilly smashing everything to bits."

"You sound reactionary."

"I realize that, and I confess I find it confusing. But what are we supposed to do? Just let everything get razed to the ground?"

"Better to be reactionary, I guess, than to usher in an age of anarchy, chaos, mob rule, another Reign of Terror . . ."

"I don't want to be reactionary. I mean, I used to *be* an anarchist! But look around, this city's embarrassing. It looks like a tsunami went through it and the only ones who've survived are meth heads, construction workers, emotional support animals, and fentanyl addicts . . ."

"I love that phrase, 'razed to the ground.' I love the way it works against itself. How the homonyms raised and razed enact the opposite gesture. One up, one down. Like the horizon."

"Any goon can raze things to the ground, any group of goons. Mob mentality has never been thought of as intelligent. Why start now? Since when did we start thinking of the mob as possessing an intelligence the rest of the population doesn't have? For some reason, we now bow to the mob, no matter who that mob is."

"Say, Bauhaus."

"Sure, if you like."

"I don't like. I find it just one more malodorous waft of the industrial age. Like Futurism or DADA, or Interstate highways. Bauhaus . . . I can't bear the starkness, the coldness, the concrete . . . it's horrible!"

"What's disturbing is that the arts for so long have found their raison d'etre in iconoclasm, in questioning institutions, in desecrating them."

"Bauhaus . . ."

". . . but it's one thing for it to happen in the arts, it's another for it to happen in society."

"You're right."

"Even the arts seem to have hit a dead end. They're eating their own tail. I heard someone at an art gallery say that non-representational art has run its course because at this point all non-representational art is actually a representation of non-representational art."

"Hmm . . . that *is* confusing."

"You can't just systematically engage in a dismantling of every aspect of society and not wind up in anarchy. From anarchy anything can happen, it creates a vacuum that usually leads to fascism, dictatorship, totalitarianism, if not total annihilation . . . it's terrifying actually, Munch was right to see it."

"I think he was Norwegian."

"Even if he's not a great painter, at least he could see that."

What Does a Vulture Eat in Los Feliz?

Our host said Katy Perry bought the monastery in Los Feliz . . . Was it Katy Perry? Katy Perry or some other famous singer who also happened to be Catholic. She was pretty sure it was Katy Perry.

"But get this," she said, "a group of nuns used to own it, and at the same time Katy Perry bought the monastery from one of the nuns, one of the other nuns sold it to someone else."

"Wait, what?" someone said.

We could see the monastery from her backyard, where we climbed up some stairs to a little terraced patio. Our host had made a pitcher of prosecco and watermelon. She carried the pitcher and glasses on a tin tray up the stairs to a table where we all sat down.

"One of nuns sold it to Katy Perry, and another nun sold it to someone else. Now there's a big scandal, a dispute as to who owned it at the time of the sale, and who had the authority to sell it. That was five years ago. It's unclear now who owns it, since two parties bought it. It's been under litigation. Everyone's talking about it. Meanwhile, the monastery's just sitting there empty, abandoned. It's been that way for years."

"Weird."

A delivery driver arrived then with our lunch, and someone ran down to get it.

"And get this," our host continued, "now the city wants it. Since it's been empty all this time. The city's claiming it's a public health issue, I guess. A nuisance. They want to turn it into a park or museum or something."

We were looking up at the monastery when the food arrived: a box of burritos and Caesar salad. Also chips and salsa and a bowl of antipasto. Clay plates with a different flower printed in half-relief on each were passed around.

"This punch is fantastic," someone said. Our host smiled.

"Love these plates," someone else said.

"I know aren't they great . . . they're from Oaxaqueños."

"I knew it!"

We ate our lunch and looked out across the valley, at the monastery on the hill. A tall iron fence and brown stucco wall ran the length of the property. The roof was tiled in typical mission style, and there were huge pine trees growing on the property, and palms, yucca, Italian cypress and agave. There was something both Tuscan and Mexican Revival about it. Same as the food we were eating.

"The whole city is waiting to see who wins," our host said, "but especially Los Feliz. If Katy Perry wins, we'll be able to see her from here. Nolan has a telescope. And there's a pool. A pool in the monastery! Can you believe it?"

"Who puts a pool in a monastery?"

"Nuns, I guess."

The table was half-shaded by a small guava tree. There were hibiscus bushes on the north edge of the property, screening the house "where Karen Gillan lives." Our host was disappointed we didn't know her. "Really? The Big Short? The Circle?" There was a garden shed that they didn't use standing against the south side of the property, near the stairs. Richard Armitage used to live in that house, "back when the *Hobbit* movies were big."

"Wait, was he the hobbit?"

"No . . ." disappointed again, "he was one of the dwarves." It was an unkempt, terraced backyard. No pool.

"This punch really is fantastic," someone said. Our host smiled again.

"Do you think she skinny dips?"

"Katy Perry?"

"Of course she skinny dips! Why not?"

"But in a monastery? It seems sort of sacrilegious."

"God doesn't mind skinny dipping."

"Not if it's Katy Perry . . . because she's Catholic."

"But what about the nuns? Will she keep the nuns? Maybe as servants?"

"That's sick. Of course not . . . besides, the nuns are all gone."

"Where'd they go?"

"I don't know. I think they were shipped off to northern California somewhere. To a monastery outside San Francisco."

"How much does it cost to ship a nun?"

"Okay, seriously: this punch is fantastic!" Our host smiled again.

A vulture glided over the valley, between us and the monastery, rocking side to side. We all saw it, and we all watched it for a while before someone said,

"What does a vulture eat in Los Feliz?"

"Don't know . . . bunnies? prairie dogs, garbage?"

We kept watching as it glided over, tilting unsteadily, like a poorly made paper airplane, then it would correct itself, then rock side to side again. It lifted in a heat vent, spiraling, rising up above the hill and over the monastery, where it seemed to pause, circling there above it.

". . . or nuns maybe, maybe they eat nuns."

". . . maybe they eat celebrities."

". . . naked celebrities."

". . . naked B-list celebrities."

"You have to tell me how you made this punch," someone said. Our host smiled.

"I think I'd like to be a vulture in LA."

"Totally."

"Wait, is Katy Perry the one who sings 'All I Wanna Do Is Have Some Fun'?"

Marguerite Duras Is Lucky She's Dead

"Telephones, and all the other agonies of life, really only keep you from doing what you ought to do."
—Imogen Cunningham

Marguerite Duras died in 1996. That was a good time to go, before this horrid century began. I mean, she hated television with a passion. She watched it all the time, but she hated its effect on the cinema, and the theatre. She would've absolutely despised the internet, the way we're trapped in our phones, how no one goes to movies or smokes cigarettes.

It was 2020 and we were getting close to the end of our first year in the pandemic. Sure we had acclimatized to a significant extent, but that didn't diminish what we'd lost. The unabatedly social interactions that used to occur every day. The grocery. The café. Stopping at a pub on the way home from work. The library. The train.

For years Liz and I would stop, late at night—after a reading or gallery or movie—at the Italian restaurant (gone now) on Broadway, where you could get a bowl of Bolognese and a glass of wine for less than ten dollars. We got to know the bartender. He filled our glasses without us asking. We learned the names of others who stopped there. One of the regulars worked at the library. He was a great reader. He knew Duras, and not just *The Lover*. He knew the essays and films and *The Sea Wall*. We talked about books, music, art, sports, the history of the city. In a word, we had a social life. We all did.

But in 2020 the trains stopped. There was no music to see, and no Italian restaurant to go to on the way home from the galleries that we no longer went to because they were closed. There was only home. Staying home. Staying home is nice when you don't have to stay home, but when you have to stay home, it's horrible.

In 2020, even if you did stop at a bar (there were a few open), you had to have your mask on. You wouldn't sit next to anyone. You didn't want to breathe or speak. You didn't want to catch the disease. But mostly you didn't want to be in this century, the 21st. You wanted to go back, or forward maybe. Anywhere but here. Preferably to a time when Marguerite Duras was complaining about the television and how it had ruined society. That was a great time, a great time to be alive.

III.

GOING TO MUSEUMS, GOING TO FOOTBALL GAMES

In which the author watches things, and watches people watching things

The Flower Seller

We went to the art museum, the big one downtown. They finally re-
opened it after a year of quarantine. What were all those pretty paintings doing in there unseen? Were they falling in the forest of other
paintings? Did they make a sound? Were they preening for each other,
satisfying the exhibitionist nature of the exhibit?

Weirdly, one of the last places we went before the pandemic, before things shut down, was the museum. To see a special exhibition of
Georgia O'Keeffe. I admit I've always had a hard time appreciating her
work, but it was nice to see her "music" pieces, and listen to them, to
see what they sounded like: this one sounds like Chopin, this one Bill
Evans' "Theme from *Spartacus*." Alli said one looked like ABBA. To each
our own set of references, I guess. We can only see what we already
know. It was obvious we were projecting. That each of us had different music playing in our heads. I suppose the paintings allowed us to
realize that. That must be worth something.

It's rare to be thrown into the vast unknown, as soon as you are it
starts closing up again. Associations and recognitions will drag even
the most sublime experience quickly to the ground. It must be a sur-
vival skill, to tamp down our sense of wonder. We can't be in awe all
the time, otherwise we'd be eaten by the thing we're in awe of. The
terror of the pandemic itself lasted only a few months. A few weeks
before people started dismissing it as just another phenomenon in an
endless string of unimpressive phenomena. I suppose that's what happens when you live in a world that contains belugas and star-nosed

moles, mosquito eaters and passionflower vines. There's just too much miracle, too much that's incomprehensible. Eventually you become ho-hum about it all.

The O'Keeffes eventually grew quiet too, and I went looking for *The Flower Seller*—a minor painting by a minor painter, but one I like to visit. Its pathos are superb (auto-correct here tells me to write "Its pathos is superb" but I just can't do it). Its pathos are superb. What was she doing all year while the museum was shut down? Selling her flowers in the dark? No one passing by to pity her, or rue the rich theatre-goers in the background.

When I got to the spot where she'd always been hanging, I found that she was on loan. A little plaque indicated the situation. Oh well. I moved on to Bonnard—an interior, *Woman at a Table*, I think—but it wasn't the same. Not the same as *The Flower Seller*. Not even close. There was no emotion in it. In the colors of the paint there was some emotion, sure. They were warm—reds, oranges, yellows—but not profoundly warm. I suppose the woman at the table was sad. I felt sad looking at it anyway, but not profoundly sad. Not in a stimulating way. It mostly made me feel claustrophobic. I was happy not to be in that room in the painting, at that table, with that woman all red and yellow and orange. It was difficult enough just to look at it.

I admit I started to panic, and turned away. Some paintings will do that to you. Some things (even some paintings) don't want to be seen. Perhaps they're not exhibitionists. Fortunately, I was able to lose myself in a marble sculpture of a child's head by Renoir, I think, or someone who wanted to be mistaken for Renoir. The *Woman at a Table* faded, and so did *The Flower Seller*. I thought of Gertrude Stein's "before the flowers of friendship faded, friendship faded." Such a lovely little playful turn of phrase. The way sometimes things fade before the symbols and behaviors of those things fade.

That's sort of what happened as my first marriage fell apart. No one there to hear it fall. Just us, two trees in a forest of misery. There was a rose vine climbing on the building across the street from where we lived. One summer, early on in our relationship, I picked one and brought it back to her. And every summer after that, I did the same. I brought her flowers long after the sentiment held meaning. The flowers themselves seemed to want to be given. So I kept giving them.

And then I didn't. Then one summer I didn't. And the next I didn't. I stopped giving her flowers and she never said a thing.

You're Not a Woman Again

We were in the museum looking at various ancient Roman artifacts. We weren't in Rome. We were in the Rome Room at the museum. The artifacts were encased in plexiglass cubes. We like to go to the Rome Room after we see whatever exhibits are happening in the main galleries. It's somehow grounding. I can't explain it, I just notice that that's what we do. Every time we go to the museum.

We were having some sort of fight, this particular time. In fact, we were having a fight we'd had several times. A hundred times. About the baby. A baby. The baby I didn't want but she did. Not that I didn't want the baby, I just didn't want to go out of our way to have it. The baby. If it happened, great. If not, well . . . I didn't like having this fight because every time we had it we arrived at an impasse. The same impasse. Nothing was resolved. It was baffling to me that we kept having it. The fight. The less we had the baby, the more we had the fight. The fight seemed to have a mind of its own. The fight was having us.

"You don't understand," she always said, "you're not a woman."

This was her coup de grâce, and I learned that it was best not to respond to this. I learned that early on, many fights ago. The hard way. So this time I didn't respond. Again.

We were standing in front of an amphora. I think it was Greek, or maybe Etruscan, despite the fact that we were in the Rome Room. The amphoras were used to store oil or wine. I was thinking it would take a lot of wine to fill up one of the amphoras. Did the wine they drank back then taste like the wine we drink now? I started to crave a glass of wine. The painting running around the amphora was odd. I didn't recognize the scene.

"What is this? Dionysus?" I asked.

"You think everything's Dionysus," she said, annoyed.

"Well it usually is when it's on a jug of wine," I said. "Who do *you* think it is?"

"It looks like Diana to me."

"Okay . . ." I looked more closely. She was usually right about these things. "Okay, Diana then . . . what's she doing?"

We both leaned in and slowly walked around the plexiglass, trying to decipher the scene scratched into the clay, or painted on it. It was hard to say.

"It's a bit weird, don't you think?" I said, hoping to move beyond the fight.

"I think it's a child," she said.

"Maybe the moon . . ." I said.

"Probably. She's goddess of the hunt, and of the moon, and of childbirth."

"Jeezus," I said.

"What? I didn't paint it . . ." she said.

"Can we just look at the art?" I said.

"We are looking at the art," she said, "and this is a painting of Diana, goddess of childbirth."

"Okay, fine."

She smiled sarcastically, "I'm going back to the Frankenthaler exhibit."

She left and I let her go without saying anything else. I didn't follow her. It's nicer to be alone in a museum anyway. I looked at the vase again. There was what looked like a couple (the expectant parents?) lounging in a field. Lying in the grass. The moon up above. Maybe our fight is as old as Time. Maybe if we were the couple on the vase, we could just offer Diana a lamb and be done with it. It's not like I didn't want a baby. I just didn't necessarily think it was a good idea. I thought it might even be a bad idea. We weren't trying not to. It just wasn't happening. And she was bothered by it, and I didn't care. Not that I didn't care, I just thought, oh well, there you go, it's not happening.

I walked around the vase again, the jar, the amphora. Maybe it's not a deer, I thought. I mean, it had antlers and hoofs, but the face was like a man's face. Sad. Resigned. Useless. It could be Dionysus after all. Just because she says it's Diana doesn't mean it is . . . I thought about the wine again. It would be nice to drink wine out of something like that.

I Thought Pom-Poms Had Gone Extinct

We went to a high school football game the other night. Alli plays saxophone in the band. How is it that nothing has changed in thirty years? There were cheerleaders, first of all. And they had pom-poms. Liz and I wondered if the word was related to the French "pomme," apple. We thought maybe. It seemed to make some sense. A pom-pom is sort of shaped like an apple. It made it more interesting to think of the girls smashing apples together and yelling.

The boys on the field, they were hurting each other. On purpose. Several limped off. One was carried off, and one left the stadium in an ambulance. For what? That seemed to be the question that had no answer. It all seemed overly dramatic, pointlessly dangerous, and ridiculously put on.

From a purely performative perspective, it was spectacular of course. A spectacle of richness and variety. There were endless dramas playing out on the field, in the band, in the student section, everywhere.

Two students climbed up to the highest part of the stadium to make out. A man and woman had an argument near us. A drunk woman cheered a little too loudly for her son. We even saw a bat swoop down from the rafters and pluck a moth out of the air. All of this was going on while the skyline of the city rose up over the stadium bleachers in the distance. It was indeed spectacular. You couldn't stage a more definitive spectacle. And we were there, part of it.

On the other side of the stadium was the opposing team. The bleachers on the other side of the field—literally, spatially, opposing us—belonged to the opposing team's fans, their cheerleaders, their cheerleader's pom-poms, and the opposing team itself—The Crusaders. How dramatic! How terrifying! The Crusaders! They had God on their side, while we were merely Bulldogs. How could we possibly stand a chance? We didn't. We lost. But we tried! We measly Bulldogs with only our powerful, protruding lower jaws, our broad chests and our flat wrinkled faces. The band played, the boys sacrificed their lives, their bones and ankles and brains, the cheerleaders cheered, and the student section roared sophomoric imprecations into the cold night air.

When we got home, our ears still ringing, we all wondered what had happened. What was it all for? A spectacle without a cause. A celebration of sorts. A ritual, a rite, primitive and instinctual, one inherent in every culture: dance, music, war . . . and always the young lovers who sneak away into the darkness, away from the scene, to ensure the ritual continues.

The next morning I looked up pom-pom in the OED. It's not an apple but a flower, a chrysanthemum. And before that (from the 1740s), a little ball of shreds and rags worn on the head.

JESUS WAS A THRASHER

My daughter and I were staring at the painting for a while. Not because it was a great painting, it wasn't, but because we were tired. We'd been at the museum for a few hours already. They didn't have a café. We were exhausted, so we found an empty bench and sat down. The bench just happened to face the painting we were staring at.

"It would be better," I said, "if they put the benches by windows, or in front of a black wall, so you could take a break from *looking*."

But the bench was in front of the painting: a nativity scene. I didn't recognize the artist. The baby, Christ, was on some blankets on the ground. He had his hands up, as if to push Mary away. Joseph was in the background, near a barn. Joseph was also looking at the baby. Everyone was, even the donkey and the chickens seemed to be eyeing the child. There were some angels (also babies) hovering above the barn. They were looking at the baby, too. But the baby, weirdly, didn't seem very happy, didn't seem very "Christ-like." A beam of sunlight illuminated the fat rolls on his arms and legs.

"It's weird that Jesus was a baby," Alli said. She was 15 at the time, no longer a baby. "Why wouldn't God just make him a man? Why did he have to make him a baby first?"

"No idea," I said.

"Like Jesus had to go to school, and be a teenager, and do homework . . ."

I shook my head.

"Do you think he played an instrument?" she said

"No idea," I said, and looked around to see if anyone could hear us, "you mean like the saxophone?"

My daughter played the saxophone. "Yeah."

"Don't know," I said, "but I think you're projecting a little bit. Do you have a Jesus complex or something?"

"No," she said, "but I bet he would've killed on the saxophone. He wouldn't even have to practice."

We were quiet for a few minutes. Both of us went on staring at the painting. "It *is* weird to think of him as a teenager, though." she laughed. "He looks weird. He's so white, and fat. And even though he's a baby, his face looks like a man's face."

I shook my head and looked around again. No one was near us. "I feel like I should point out that that's not Jesus, it's just a rendering of Jesus. An interpretation of a story about Jesus."

"I bet Jesus would be one of the popular kids," she said.

"You mean like in the lunchroom?"

"Yeah. I bet he'd sit with the skaters. I don't think he'd sit with the jocks, but he'd probably sit with the skaters . . ."

"Don't know," I said, "I haven't seen any paintings of Jesus at a skate park."

"Yeah . . . why is he always a baby? Or dead? Or eating dinner? They never show him as a teenager."

"No idea," I said, "I guess there aren't any stories of him as a teenager . . ."

"I'd actually like to hear some stories about Jesus as a teenager."

"Like who did he ask to prom?"

"Yeah, and did he study for his SATs or just take them, commando."

"Commando? Without underwear?"

". . . without studying."

"I think he probably studied," I said, but she ignored me.

". . . and why are the angels always in the background? And nobody seems to notice? If there were angels in real life everyone would be like 'oh my god look there's some angels on the roof of the barn,' and everyone would look at them. They wouldn't just ignore them like 'oh yeah, there's those fucking angels on the roof of the barn again.' "

"Hey . . ."

"What?"

"Don't say 'fucking.' "

"You say it all the time."

"I know, but still . . . I don't say it about angels."

We looked at the painting for a few more minutes. It *was* a weird painting. The subject wasn't the only problem. The light and shadows didn't always make sense. And the scale of Joseph by the barn made it seem like he was ten feet tall. It was a strange choice to put the bench in front of this particular painting. Or to hang this painting in front of the bench.

"Can we find another place to sit?" Alli said.

"Why?" I was tired and didn't really want to move.

"They're creepy."

"Who?"

"You know," she said, and gestured toward the painting.

"The fucking angels?"

"Hey! You can't say it if I can't say it."

We looked at them for a few more seconds. "They are pretty creepy," I said, and we left.

Portrait of My Wife with Modern Landscape

We were in the gallery. In separate parts of the gallery. We always start out together but then drift apart. Nothing's said. It just happens. Every time. It's better to look at art alone, anyway.

She tends to linger over each painting. In order, one after another. I tend to wander around until something catches my eye, and then I stare for a while, letting what's there reveal itself. Neither way is necessarily better than the other. We're just different.

This time was the same. I can't remember the exhibit. Modern Landscapes, I think. We'd been there a half-hour or so. Nothing much had caught my eye.

It was a small gallery. I walked through the entire show, which was arranged in a circle of rooms. When I got to the end, I saw her standing at the beginning. She had her notebook out. She was scribbling something down.

She likes to take notes. In fact, she's a compulsive notetaker. Once, a friend gave us tickets to the opera, *Tristan et Iseult*. The lights went out and Iseult started singing for Tristan. It was very beautiful and tragic and I suppose I was unprepared for it. I was overwhelmed. I reached for my wife's hand there in the dark of the theatre, and there in the dark of the theatre I found my wife's hand writing in her notebook.

"Sorry," she whispered, and patted my hand, then continued writing her notes. Fine, I thought, I'll hold my own hand. And I did.

Anyway, I saw her standing there, looking at the very first painting in the gallery and taking notes. She wore the long, cream-colored coat that had been her great-great aunt's. She always looks elegant when she wears it. The way women are so elegant in film noir: always tall and thin and concealing something. I walked behind her so that I could see what she was looking at. What she might be finding at that moment. What was notable. What she was seeing in that particular painting that she found noteworthy.

The painting was a landscape from someplace that reminded me of Palm Springs. Not that I've ever been to Palm Springs. It reminded me of what I imagine Palm Springs looks like. At least, a road outside of Palm Springs. It reminded me of Brett Easton Ellis. A desert road lined on both sides with palm trees that diminished into the painting, away from the viewer, who in this instance, was us, my wife and me. The parallel lines converged as they receded to a vanishing point, which seemed purposefully simplistic. Outside the line of trees, on the right, was a sign that read, CAR WASH, in pink, neon letters. The car wash itself was beneath it. A few cars were painted crudely, and a man in dark clothes was merely gestured at, sketched in, nothing more than a few dark lines. The sky was enormous. Mostly blue but mottled here and there with white.

The overall feel was one of loneliness. There was humor, to be sure. The CAR WASH was absurd. I guess that's what struck me: the overwhelming sadness of the thing, the thing that was both a landscape and a portrait of the condition of humanity. That dark figure alone in the middle of the desert washing cars. For what reason? For what purpose? The longer I looked, the more depressed I became. Maybe not depressed, but filled with despair. A sense of futility, void of hope.

And in front of it, scribbling hurriedly, as if she were a court stenographer from the nineteenth century, was my wife—enlivened, inspired—on whom the painting was evidently having the opposite effect.

A Note on My Favorite Painting in One of the Shitty Museums in My Town; or, It Could've Been a Plant

A portrait of Bianca Maria Sforza hangs in the atrium at one of the shitty art museums in my town. Most people walk past it without stopping to look. It's unexceptional, or rather, exceptional only for the sad, sour look on the sitter's face. The painting is merely "art," as in, "we need to get some art for this atrium." It could be anything. And it is.

Because of this, it's one of my favorite paintings in the entire museum. A small museum, sure, and one that's far too self-conscious. Some museums have become enormously worried about how they will appear to the public. Are our politics right? Are we offending anyone? Having no clear vision of their own what to show, these curators try instead to guess at what their patrons might want to see, in a feckless display of flaccid imagination. What's the point of a curator at all? May as well have the general public fill out a questionnaire. Democracy now! No matter that the general public cares very little for aesthetic values. Who cares about aesthetics in a world of perpetual social crisis?

The portrait of Bianca Maria Sforza is an afterthought. It is thoughtless, nearly unintentional. It's mere decoration. Less an *objet d'art* than an *objet trouvé*, an object to fill a space. They just needed something on the wall. They found a painting. It could've been a plant, or a coat rack. I love it!

I've come to appreciate this type of accidental, thoughtless display. It's far better than what passes these days as thoughtful intention, certainly when that thoughtful intention is meant only to cater to a public that has no sense of art, no faith in art, in fact despises art, and thinks art should have the subservient role only of reinforcing certain moral values and very little (if anything) else. Essentially, a public who believes that the best art is the art that least resembles art at all.

The Flower Seller Again; or, Why Are Mediums Always So Happy?

I was thinking about *The Flower Seller* again, a painting by Jules Bastian-Lepage in our local museum. Well, it used to be in our local museum, for years in fact, but now it's disappeared. I'm not sure if they loaned it to another museum or just put it in storage. I miss it. I used to visit it like you'd visit a friend, not a great friend but a friend nonetheless. It was always nice to see it.

The painting is sentimental and didactic. It depicts a pathetic street urchin, a beautiful young girl, who is selling flowers. In the background, pompous socialites lurk ominously in the shadows. One of the socialites seems to see the girl and looks annoyed, if not disgusted. The painting tells us what we're supposed to feel and think. We sympathize with the girl, with her poverty. We despise the socialites, and their wealth.

The painting is bad. But for some inexplicable reason, I like it.

Marguerite Duras has two essays about flower sellers in her collection *Outside*. They're not really essays. "Studies" is perhaps a better word. The one entitled "Paris Rabble" is a kind of character sketch about an old woman, aged 71, who sells flowers illegally in the spring, summer and fall. In the winter, when there are no flowers to sell, she makes her living as a thief. She is on public assistance, but it's not enough. She spends her winters in jail. It's warm in jail. She doesn't mind. She's a poor thief but a good mother. She's birthed eleven children; seven of them are still alive. She's raised her children so well that they don't want anything to do with her, with their vagrant mother.

The other sketch—"The Algerian's Flowers"—is a kind of anti-colonialist fantasy. It concerns a young Algerian immigrant in Paris, who also sells flowers illegally. He works just down the street from the Buci market. He has a small cart. The police see him and ask for his papers. He has none. The cops flip his cart over and laugh. The flowers fly everywhere. The intersection "fills with the flowers of early spring, Algerian spring."

What's interesting to me is how flat the Duras sketches are in comparison to the Lepage painting. The painting is full of sentiment and pity. So much sentiment, in fact, that it is a bad painting. While the Duras sketches are so lacking in sentiment that they come across as bad writing. Are we to pity these characters that the author treats so weirdly, as if she doesn't know what to do with them herself? They are like objects she's found in the street. She picks them up and looks at them. "Hm. Look at that," she seems to say. This is reportage. Not editorializing. This is the bowl of fruit. Not the still life.

The writing is bad, and yet she would be wrong to linger. In the foreword to *Outside*, Duras blames the bad writing throughout the book on the fact that she's writing for newspapers: "the writing is inevitably affected by the impatience of the medium [journalism], by the obligation to write quickly, and is somewhat neglected." She doesn't care: "the idea of neglecting the writing does not displease me."

In fact, neglecting the writing seems to save her from sentimentality. To neglect the writing is insurance against overwriting, something Lepage has had too much time to do.

FOR GODS SAKES

"Everything wrote when I was in the house writing. Writing was everywhere. It is also possible not to write, to forget a fly. To only watch it. To see how it too struggles so desperately, recorded in an unknown sky and for nothing."
—Marguerite Duras

My friend enjoys things without writing about them. I find this fascinating. Not that I live my life in order to write about it—I don't. But my friend, he just lets events go. For him they simply disappear. He remembers them, but that's it. No diary or journal entry, no poem or essay. Nothing. Just a few memories that rarely rise to the surface.

I'm not suggesting my way is better. By all accounts, my friend seems happy enough. Happier than I am in fact. His by-all-appearances-positive attitude is enviable.

He's married. Has two grown kids. He's retired now and financially secure. He and his wife travel: Japan, the Dordogne, Mexico, Ireland. He loves his cat. Goes fishing. Crabbing. Rides his bike to the pub . . . He writes about none of it.

Perhaps he's enlightened. Or perhaps he just doesn't enjoy writing. Maybe I'm too attached to this world. Maybe I'm trying too hard to slow it down as it slips quickly out from under me, from within me. I admire his lack of anxiety. His lack of urgency. He doesn't write a single thing! He does crossword puzzles for gods sakes! And he does them calmly, as if it isn't a supreme waste of time.

I'm afraid that when I'm in my sixties all I'll be doing is writing. Frantically writing. Sitting in a chair somewhere, desperately taking notes on what I see out the window, cataloguing as many memories as possible: the dogwood leaves turning orange, a rain just beginning, the neighbor who moved into the apartment across the street after Kevin left, the circumstances of Kevin's leaving, someone else named Kevin taking his place. I'm afraid I'll be another Henry Darger madly documenting the instances where the weatherman got the weather wrong, even if only by a degree or two.

What weird narcissism is this? That stares out and documents the brick buildings, the gray sky, the workers removing the telephone pole where the little girl named Naima used to live.

"Like the Coltrane song," I said when I met Naima's parents, but they didn't know the reference. "She's not named after the song?"

"No, we just liked the name . . ."

"Do you still like it?"

"Yes, of course. What do you mean?"

"I don't know . . . I'm not sure. You said 'liked,' so . . ."

"She's our daughter. Of course we still like the name."

They avoided me after that interaction. I'm not sure exactly why. It seemed like a logical question given their choice of words. For some reason, this kind of thing often happens to me.

Wrought iron rails wrap around my friend's front balcony, geraniums spill down in brilliant platitudes. By fall they're wasted, neglected for weeks, mostly dead, brown and leggy, hanging over the gutters in the cold evening air. None of it bothers him.

I love my friend. I confess, I'm weirdly jealous. He is living a literal life, simple and direct, whereas I can't escape the metaphors. I see myself in everything, in everything some part of me (usually my mortality). Every instance is both that instance and the symbolic representation of other instances.

We go to a gallery, my life hangs on every wall, and it *is* every wall, and it is also the gallery itself, a showcase of impressions, a thing in which to hang other things, a place to hang *from*. My friend sees none of it. He has a great time. He spends no more than a few seconds on each painting. He smiles, laughs, suggests we go for a beer.

At the pub we talk about the paintings . . . I could speak on them for hours, but he says only, "I liked them. They were nice." He's not interested. What he's interested in is the present moment: the beer, the mirror hanging over the bar, and the young couple arguing at a small table in the corner. All of which he'll forget, and I'll write down in a notebook tomorrow. For whom? For what? I have no idea.

IV.

READING

In which the author goes to jail,
and argues that no one reads anymore

My Favorite Book

The last time I was in jail it was November. I was twenty-seven. The streets were wet and from the cell that I was in you could see the mist beading on the windows of the cars parked down below.

It wasn't a cell really. It was a big room on the 13th floor of a skyscraper jail. It wasn't a cell at all. It was a holding tank: the drunk tank. It was a fish tank for drunks, and it's true it was difficult to breathe. The rain and gray light through the narrow, metal-reinforced windows added to the claustrophobia in the tank, the sense of drowning. All the fish wore orange prison clothes. It was a goldfish tank.

To be clear, I wasn't a drunk. I wasn't then and I'm not now. Sure, I had *been* drunk directly preceding my arrest, but I wasn't *a* drunk. It would be an insult to drunks if I identified as one. Something like cultural appropriation. I am no *poseur*! I was only twenty-seven, a novice, not a drunk. I had none of the telltale behaviors a drunk exhibits. I didn't drink, for instance, in the morning (unless I'd been drinking all night and morning just happened to come around).

It was the only jail I've ever been in that had windows the prisoners could look out. I suppose that sounds humane, to have windows to look out of, but after I noticed I could see the café on 2nd and Jackson, the one I used to go to when I worked downtown, after I noticed that, I stopped looking out the window at the world that was now shut off from me. It wasn't humane, it was cruel.

I had been in jail enough times to know that you could ask for books. When the food trays came, I asked a guard, very quietly, if he could get me one. In jail, people who read are considered, well, gay. I don't usually mind when people think I'm gay (it does happen, I grew up in southern Indiana, where they also think you're gay if you read), but jail isn't exactly the best place to be thought of that way.

The Bible might be the only book you can read in jail and not be thought of as gay.

"A book?" the guard said, suspiciously.

"Yes, please."

"What kind of book?"

"Anything is fine."

"Like the Bible?"

"Sure, if that's all you have, but really anything's fine."

The guard seemed to think about it for a while, and then said, "I'll see what I can do."

I never saw him again.

A few hours later a different guard opened the door.

"Walton!"

Walton means essentially, "foreigner," and in jail I never felt so aptly named. I was a foreigner there. Jail and southern Indiana aren't the only places I feel like a foreigner—there's also the mall, social media, and planet earth. I'm guessing a few others also felt like foreigners in the drunk tank, but I wouldn't have known. I tried not to talk to anyone if I could help it. Jail isn't exactly, for me anyway, my preferred place to make friends. Talking to people in jail is generally considered . . . well, you get the picture. In jail everyone is afraid everyone else is either gay or will think they're gay. It's about as gay-friendly as a NASCAR race.

"Walton!"

As I walked over to the door, I thought maybe I was being released. Perhaps someone had bailed me out. But who? I didn't call anyone to tell them I was in jail. I was trying to think who might have found out I was there. I purposely didn't tell my girlfriend, for fear she might dump me, which she did anyway. Maybe she found out somehow, and overcame her shock and disappointment to forgive me and bail me out. I was thinking how wonderful she was, what a forgiving gesture it was, when I got to the door.

"You wanted a book?" the guard said.

"Ahh," I said, disappointed not to be released, "yes, please."

"Will this do?" he slid a book through the slot in the steel door. I didn't recognize the title, or author, but it was a book and I couldn't care less what kind of book it was. The fact that it wasn't the Bible was a relief. I just needed to read, to escape. I wasn't looking for moral instruction or origin stories. I was well aware of how I wound up there. In jail.

The book he handed me was some sort of mystery or thriller. I could tell by the overtly symbolic objects arranged on the cover—a seal or stamp of some kind, white gloves—and the font dripping blood.

"Yes, perfect, thanks."

I walked back over to my bunk, of which my bed took up the lower half. The upper half was occupied by an enormous man who barely fit into his orange outfit. He was lying on his side, looking at me, I lowered my eyes and looked at the book. When I got to my bunk, I crawled under his fat belly, which hung like a curtain over the side. Every time the food trays came, this man grunted and huffed and coughed a phlegmy cough as he climbed down from above. His huge, fat stomach flapping down the rungs of the ladder. I tried not to make eye contact with him, or his stomach, or any part of anyone else for that matter.

I read that book cover to cover. And then started reading it again. I was chain-reading, hotboxing it. I never left my bed the rest of the time I was there. Three days it turned out. I stopped eating. I refused my food tray. My bunkmate noticed and asked if he could eat it. "Yes." He traded my whole tray one night for a cigarette butt someone had somehow smuggled in. I tried not to wonder how they'd done it, and how it must've tasted when my bunkmate smoked it.

Sometimes now I think about buying that book, or checking it out from the library. I sort of miss it. Not that I miss it, I guess, it's hard to explain. It's like if you were drowning and someone threw you one of those round flotation devices. You might want to hang that in your living room, something like a memento mori, I guess.

It was one of the most important books I've ever held in my hands.

The Perfect Reader

I don't like to tell people what I'm reading. It seems pretentious. I don't really like to talk about books at all. At least not with most people. Certainly not with other writers! The best people to talk about books with are people who don't write, who only read.

Of course, there are people who only read to "better themselves." I don't like those people. How could I? They ask you what you're reading in the same way they ask you what your politics are. For them there are certain books that are "right," and certain books that are "wrong." They only read the books in fashion. And by "in fashion" I mean in political fashion, in socio-cultural fashion. They're hipsters. They refuse to read Whitman. It's disgusting.

Of course, I talk about books with my wife. She is a writer, and she's also my wife (that's two strikes against her). We have to talk about books, as, like most married people, we are constantly trying to find things that are interesting to talk about.

And sometimes, because we live together, one of us will just start talking and the other one will overhear, and the person talking will sometimes be talking about books. We are lucky in that we mostly read different things. But not always. Sometimes we read the same things . . . sometimes we read the same things on purpose! This can be, at best, interesting. At worst we argue for hours about whether the language of Choderlos de La Clos is too florid, the sentimentality of Maggie Nelson is too cloying, or if Pascal's *Pensées* are the greatest justification of Christian belief ever compiled or a kind of La Rochefoucauld-ian satire on human folly.

"Why does he go on and on about Jesus? It's insufferable," I say.

"So what?" she says, "It's no big deal. They're *pensées*."

"And?"

"And nothing. It's just that, they're *pensées*. *Pensées* means thoughts. They're just thoughts. Mere thoughts. Pascal can think whatever he likes."

"Well, sometimes I wish he'd keep his thoughts to himself!"

"I'm sure the same has been said about you . . ."

"What's that supposed to mean?"

"Nothing."

Our arguments become memes, and inevitably personal. And because we are both writers, we insult not only the other's intelligence, but by extension their writing as well. Now, insulting a writer's intelligence is not that big of a deal in and of itself. They don't really care. But if you insult their writing they will sulk for weeks!

She told me about an idea for a personal essay / literary collage she was considering writing and I dumbly remarked that there should be a genre called "stylized memoirs by writers with nothing to say." She didn't speak to me for a month.

A few months later, she accused me (somewhat accurately) of more or less the same thing. Touché.

The only literary things we have ever agreed on are three: that Dostoevsky's Svidrigalov is perhaps the most perfect villain in all of literature, that MFA programs have ruined poetry (they "have made a papier mâché of poetry") and that, in America, we've hardly advanced past the works of Emily Dickinson and Walt Whitman. Regarding anything else, we will argue for days.

My friend Susan, I think, is the perfect reader. First of all, she doesn't write. Secondly, she is endlessly patient. She's read William Gass' fiction for gods sakes! She doesn't seem to form snap judgements or let her ego intercede in the story. She just watches it happen. She lets the story happen to her. It's very passive, and that may be the best way to read: to surrender completely to the writer. After all, a book is not a conversation, it's an argument, a proposition. You can only have conversations *about* a book, not *with* it. In fact, I think that's why a lot of writers write in the first place. We can say whatever we want without anyone talking back to us. By the time a reader does talk back, we've already stopped talking and moved onto something else.

The best way to read a book is to just let it happen to you. Pay attention, yes, but don't resist it. The time for objections comes when the text is done. Pascal couldn't care less what I think of his "*pensées*."

The Opposite of Funny

"I read your book," she said.

"Oh great," I said.

"I really liked it."

"Thanks."

"I didn't understand it," she said, "but I really liked it."

"Okay?" I said.

"You know you're very funny."

"Mmm . . ."

"Do you think I'm funny?" she said.

"Um, yeah, I guess, mom. You're pretty funny," I said.

"I don't think I'm funny. Your father's funny."

"Oh yeah?"

"Of course, he's not very funny anymore." she said.

"No?" I said.

"No," she said, "he's mostly just tired now. 'Honey where's my beer? Where's the remote? Are we eating tonight? Can we turn the channel now?' That's about all he says anymore. He hardly gets up out of his chair."

"That's not very funny at all," I said.

"No," she said, "it's the opposite of funny."

"That's too bad," I said.

"What's the opposite of funny?"

"I don't know," I said, "maybe boring or sincere? Maudlin?"

"What's that?" she said.

"What's what?"

"Maudlin."

"It's like overly sincere, or sentimental. It actually comes from Mary Magdalen weeping."

"What comes from Mary Magdalen weeping?"

"Maudlin."

"I don't know what you're talking about, honey," she said, "maybe it's just not funny."

"Maybe what's just not funny?"

"Maybe that's what the opposite of funny is: just not funny."

"Ah, I see," I said, "I suppose that works fine."

"Your father," she said.

"My father what?" I said.

". . . is the opposite of funny."

"I wouldn't know," I said.

"No, I guess not," she said, "you should talk to him sometime."

"Sure," I said.

"You know he's not doin nothin, he just sits in his chair."

"Great."

"I don't think it's that great . . . you should call him sometime."

"Sure."

"I did like your book though."

"Thanks," I said.

"You should write one that I can understand sometime."

"Stop saying that."

"I'm sorry," she said.

"You don't have to be sorry," I said, "just stop saying that. What's there to understand?"

"I don't know, I guess. Maybe that's why I don't understand it."

"Jeezus," I said.

"But I did like it," she said.

"Thanks," I said.

"You should send it to your cousin Erika. She's real smart. She would understand it."

"Uh huh," I said.

"She's a college professor," she said.

"Yes, I remember."

"I don't understand what it is she really teaches, but I'm sure she's real smart."

"Women's Studies," I said.

"Yes," she said, "I think so."

"Have you heard from her?"

"No," she said, "but I see her on Facebook. You know she wrote a book, too?"

"Really?"

"Yep, Uncle Bill sent it to me."

"Great," I said, "did you read it?"

"I did," she said.

"And?" I said.

"I really liked it."

"Great."

"I didn't understand it, but I really liked it."

What We Love About Artists Are Their Behavioral Disorders

In the 1960s Joan Didion carried a typewriter around with her when she flew on assignments, flew to vacation destinations, flew to visit friends. She carried it in cabs to the airport, lugged it to her gate, had it on her lap on the plane. She carried two legal pads and pens as well, but more importantly, she carried a typewriter. Why? "To start typing the day's notes."

There's something wildly excessive about this. Especially seen from the 21st century. I have a manual typewriter. I don't carry it anywhere. It's heavy. It's on a shelf by a few bottles of liquor, gifted liquor, liquor we will probably never drink: Maraschino liqueur, Metaxa, a mini bottle of amaro that we can't get the cap off of, Bailey's, that type of thing. I don't even remember where they came from, those bottles.

A standard portable typewriter weighs about fifteen pounds. Fifteen pounds! Didion lugged that thing around with her. Found her gate, or a table near her gate, opened the typewriter, inserted a piece of paper, and started typing. Right there in the airport.

Am I wrong to find this extravagant? Was everyone doing this? I'm sure she was on a deadline, but even so. Couldn't she have just written her notes and typed them up when she got home? It must've seemed efficient, sensible, to carry a typewriter. Perhaps it was. Perhaps there was no other way.

She was, of course, mostly writing for someone else. For *Vogue* or *Vanity Fair* or the *San Francisco Examiner*, but it still strikes me as compulsive. Perhaps all writers are compulsive. Of course they are. Why does this surprise me? Why am I only realizing that now?

Compulsion is defined as "an irresistible impulse to act, regardless of the rationality of the motivation."

Was the motivation for Didion as simple as having a deadline, or earning a paycheck? I doubt it. I mean, that was in play of course, but not to the extent that you would carry a typewriter on and off a plane.

What we love about artists and writers, as much as if not more than their work, are their behavioral disorders. I love Didion's journalism, the spare prose and provocative political asides. The unfinished, uncooked quality of *The White Album*. How those essays seem to end before they begin. I love her writing, but I love her more knowing she was once wandering around Colombia or El Salvador in huge sunglasses and a tailored skirt, carrying a purse, a cigarette, and an Olivetti typewriter that weighed as much (according to a quick google search) as a bowling ball, four bricks, or a bag of seven pineapples.

That image, to me, is as wonderful as anything she wrote.

A Good, Quick Stab in the Eye

I realize I do have a lot to say (my wife points this out frequently), but I also realize that none of it's worth very much. No more and no less, I guess, than anyone else, than the others who form opinions, judgements, etc. Liz says, "you're so judgmental!" And I: "Fantastic! that's proof that I'm a living, functioning human being." She doesn't like when I judge people, but you should hear her mezcal-fueled rants about our local art scene on any given weekend evening.

There are, of course, men and women far more intelligent than I am (including my wife), who express themselves more eloquently. I recommend you read their books. I certainly enjoy them. But why exactly, or to what end, are we reading? Reading as means to enlightenment? Self-betterment? Education? Hmm . . . Isn't all of that merely pleasure in one form or another? And isn't mere pleasure reason enough?

Liz is reading Proust . . . and has been for the last three years. We discuss it on occasion, and wonder what all that soporific dribble is worth. I think we've determined (though I'm not sure if she wholly agrees) that it is worth much if it affects you deeply, in a pleasurable way (you will have to define pleasure yourself). But, it means very little if it hardly bothers you at all. That is, if it doesn't move you at all. If it doesn't *upset* you. There's no point in reading Proust just to read Proust. If you feel like you're supposed to. If you're just checking him off your list.

I am greatly moved by the little knife wounds of Pascal, La Rochefoucauld, Porchia, Duras, Ikkyu, etc . . . I'll spare you my list of favorite authors. When people list their favorite authors, they are usually trying to appear more intelligent than they are, more interesting, more on trend, or more politically or morally righteous. I am none of these things. I don't think I'm intelligent. Certainly not more intelligent than an intelligent person. I'm something like one of those weird, unskilled Mexican clowns you see in the plazas of Guadalajara or DF. I guess I'm a Scots-Irish clown, if such a clown can exist. I like the authors I like not because I think they make me better, but because they are, for me, like acupuncture or nettle stings. I am an itch, and they are the scratch I need. They feel good to me. I enjoy their mischievous remarks. Their attempts to make sense of the world. The way they ask, each in their own way: what the hell is this place?

When it comes to books, we shouldn't ask much. Only one thing: "does it please me?" I guess I like Proust, too. But honestly, I much prefer a good quick stab in the eye to the drip drip doldrum of his asphyxiatingly ornamental excess.

Reading 1984

I read George Orwell's *1984* recently and it was torture. By torture I don't mean the actual torture in the book (of which there is much), but the torture of description. The modern human mind can no longer tolerate descriptive writing. What's the point? Where's the action? Where's the sex? (I did like the romantic interludes, Mr. Orwell, the sex scenes in the park and in the secret room above the antique store were not only sparingly described, but/and/also surprising and inspired!)

Furthermore, the highly descriptive writing in Orwell's book is describing in minute particulars a highly disturbing dystopian cityscape. Uglier than any downtown Portland Oregon in January, human zombies strewn about like scattered wares at a Goodwill donation center. The dystopian novel has saturated our times. At least it *had* saturated our times up until a few years ago, when our times became actually dystopian (life, perhaps, does indeed imitate art). In the few years preceding the pandemic it was all dystopian fiction all the time, and usually in the form of a graphic YA novel—that form that is meant for, let's be honest, those who'd rather be watching TV than reading, those who don't want to read a story but want a story to be shown to them. Reading this type of thing is not just passively allowing a text to present itself to you, it's a form of catatonic couch potato-ism that requires little more brain activity than scrolling through TikTok.

Maybe the dystopian phase has passed? I don't know, time will tell. Perhaps now we prefer a softball, politically appropriate personal essay? A confessional essay? An essay that allows the reader to become a voyeur. Is all the world a fetish? Or do we just endlessly fetishize the world? And if you're always saying the "right" thing, aren't you always saying nothing? A scream in a theatre full of screaming people isn't a scream you can hear.

Forgive me, I digress.

While reading *1984*, I was surprised at how bored I was. Maybe the fact that Orwell is English should have tipped me off (Trollope surely represents the height of boredom, despite the scandal in his name).

Or maybe boredom is the inevitable outcome of all seminal works. If you don't read the original first, and instead read the thousands of imitations of that original, the original then comes across as hackneyed. Sad. I arrived seventy years too late.

George Orwell is a nom de plume, as I'm sure you know. Orwell's real name is Eric Arthur Blair. An odd choice, to forego Eric Arthur Blair in favor of George Orwell. Eric Arthur Blair has a certain flare, but George Orwell sounds like someone who eats at a Cracker Barrel on Saturday night. You can hardly pronounce the name George Orwell without biting the side of your mouth.

Lastly, the book is also torture because of all the, well, torture. It just goes on and on and on. It's torture to read. Orwell/Blair certainly drive their point home. What's the point exactly of torturing Winston for fifty pages, almost one fifth of the book? Twenty pages of electric shock and a rat eating out Winston's eyeballs would surely have been enough. Now, I love violence just as much as the next American (I should probably confess here that I don't mind eating at Cracker Barrel on Saturday night or any other night), but don't we understand the nature of brainwashing without the rat eating out Winston's eye sockets? Don't we both understand it and yet also inexplicably succumb to it? And if we do still succumb to brainwashing and totalitarian propagandas, have we really understood? We understand and we accept, thank you very much. Please yes, march out another Trump, another Bolsonaro, another Kim Jung Un, another Putin and Meloni, we are ready and willing to partake in a little propaganda swilling—or, at least, helpless to resist it.

Perhaps I'm wrong. Maybe fifty pages of torture were too few.

I read *1984* and it was torture. The most torturously frightening notion isn't even in the book: the fact that despite the book being a scathing satire of fascism, totalitarianism, and sycophancy, we seem incapable of enacting the wisdom that it offers. Instead, we leap with arms out and brains disengaged into the cynical movements that would grind our humanity into meal.

Perhaps his pen name should've been George, Oh Well.

I GUESS THIS CONSTITUTES, TO A CERTAIN EXTENT, MY POETICS

A few years ago I decided I would read contemporary fiction. Nonfiction, too. Whatever people were talking about, as long as it was contemporary. I would stop seeking out "great" books, and read "contemporary" books, no matter the subject. No more Tolstoy, Flaubert, O'Connor. From now on, I would only read contemporary works of literature. And that's what I did. I read a lot of it, contemporary literature, over the span of a few years.

Part of this was due to the fact that my writer friends were starting to get published. And if they weren't getting published, they were starting to talk about recently published books. Some of my friends started literary presses. They were publishing other friends' books. I felt an obligation to read them. I felt an obligation to be part of the conversation.

I suppose I should say that I was never fully convinced this was a good idea. It just seemed like something I should do. Some of my friends were radically rejecting any book published more than a few years ago. *Any book!* Certainly white men were out. But also white women. Flannery O'Connor was out (she uses the N-word in her fiction). Gertrude Stein was out (too wealthy, and didn't do enough to help the French Resistance fight the Nazis). Anne Sexton was out (too WASPy, too suburban). It seemed that this trend of book burning applied to anything written prior to the American Civil Rights Movement (with the exception of very few: Frederick Douglass and [maybe] Emily Dickinson). Even the latter half of the 20th century was canceled for just about everyone not named James Baldwin, Adrienne Rich, Octavia Butler, Susan Howe, or Claudia Rankine (though weirdly Rupi Kaur was allowed to dumb the minds of readers by the millions). For a time, it seemed that every contemporary non-fiction book published had to have a quote from at least three of these authors, cited clearly and ostentatiously in the bibliography or endnotes so that all who wound up there would know exactly where the author stood (on the *correct* side of history of course).

This, as you can see, was on the political Left: in Language Arts classes at my daughter's public high school, in my wife's Master's in Teaching program, in most universities. But lest the Left have all the fun, soon the political Right was canceling books, too. They were canceling books for different reasons, but canceling, nonetheless. The Right had a lot of experience with this. But then again, so did the Left.

Sometimes both sides would cancel the same author, for different reasons! Walt Whitman, for instance, was canceled by the Left for being white, and by the Right for being gay. Brett Easton Ellis was canceled by the Right for being too radical and too gay, and by the Left for not being radical enough or gay enough. The list was long. The orgy of ostracization had reached bacchanal-like proportions! Writers like George Orwell, Kurt Vonnegut, and J.D. Salinger were canceled for being white, cis, and sexist. Surrealism and DADA were canceled for being white, cis, sexist, privileged. Susan Sontag was canceled by both sides: too literary and either not radical enough or too radical. In short, everyone was out. Not that these censors had read all these books (I'm sure some of them hadn't read any of these books), they just canceled them by association. For being on the wrong side of the tracks. The tracks, of course, being the tracks of the Woke Railroad. Wokeness being anything that questioned America, whiteness, capitalism, patriarchy, heterosexuality, colonialism, etc., anything that questioned what we used to call in the '90s "the dominant paradigm." If you were perceived to be woke, the Right canceled you. If you were not, the Left canceled you.

It got to the point that anyone and everyone was guaranteed to be canceled at some point, either for being too woke, or for not being woke enough.

It was all very confusing. I just wanted to read books. I admit, I wasn't exactly sure what the point of it all was. I suppose it was an attempt at a kind of "cultural cleanse." A cultural cleanse, at least, of the literary culture: readers, publishers, agents, booksellers, reviewers, critics (are there critics anymore?), etc. Or maybe it was just an elaborate marketing ploy, an army of agent provocateurs, and the modus operandi for these people was not cultural revolution but to sell *their* books. (A banned book, after all, is a book that sells well.)

Perhaps I'm naïve.

The last contemporary book I read was, I think, typical of a lot of books I've read over the last few years. I spent a lot of time with it. A few weeks. I even liked the book. It was great in places. Or good in places. It was fine in places. It was by turns a dismantling of American culture, and a victim narrative. I liked it, but I recognized the formula and by that, at least, I was a bit bored.

And then one morning I was looking through my bookshelves for the next thing to read, and I found . . . well, I grabbed a book of poems. Zen poems by Taigu Ryokan. Poems from Japan in the 1700s. I opened it at random:

"After walking for a time, I reach the pavilion / the sun sets behind the western mountains / willow leaves cover the little garden / the pond is cold and the witch hazel faded . . ."

I closed the book.

I guess I was shocked in a way, by how quiet Ryokan's sentences were. How simple. How humane. How lacking in ego. How lacking in theory. How simply descriptive. How lovely the lovely music. How the translator let "little garden" echo "western mountains" and "the pavilion," so that by the time we reach the "witch hazel faded" we feel as if it rhymes, even though it doesn't. What was this? What was I reading?

The language of the poem was so direct, so immediate. So true. By true I guess I mean that you can believe the author knows what he's talking about. Has seen it, reflected on it, digested it, and offered his understanding of it to us. Nothing special, I suppose. Things in the world one can see when one is alive, if we're lucky. And we *are* lucky.

Maybe you had to be there. Maybe you have to experience it yourself. Maybe you had to read contemporary books for a few years to appreciate Ryokan? I wasn't sure. I was, in fact, confused.

I opened the book again. At random. I was a little worried that I would be disappointed this time. What I'd read was perfect. Why read more? But I couldn't help myself. I was starved, malnourished from so many years of, well, noise. I opened the book and read:

"If you speak delusions, everything becomes delusion. If you speak truth, everything becomes truth."

I closed it again. Again humiliated. Knowing that I speak delusion, almost entirely delusion. That all of us so often do. Hopefully, the realization of that, we never cancel. Though part of me fears that we already have.

On Being Alive

The mornings were cold and dark again. It was Sunday. I was up at 6. Not for any particular reason. Not for work, I mean. Or to help Alli off to school. But because I felt I had to get up early, just to be alive. As if that was my job—being alive—and I had to get to it.

So I woke up at 6. Showered. Made myself a cup of coffee. Walked to the chair by the window. Read. I read. I watched the sky slowly grow light. Or become light. I wondered what the proper verb should be. Fade to light? Pale to light? Lighten? Anyway, I watched the sky change from black to blue to grey. And I read.

Was I alive? I guess so.

People outside were jogging, or leaving their apartments to go to work, or the market, or whatever it is people do on a Sunday. One man coughed uncontrollably, and then spat in the garden. He looked homeless. Or maybe had a home but was an addict? Maybe mentally ill? Maybe all three, I'm not sure. Was he more alive than I was? He seemed like he had something to do. He was going places. Where I have no idea, but he was definitely going somewhere. I was sitting on the couch. I was reading Dorothy Parker.

I put the book down. "I'll get dressed," I thought. "I'll go for a walk. I'll spit in the garden."

But I didn't move. I watched as a squirrel ran across the road. The squirrel seemed anxious. Urgent. There was no traffic, but he was running fast to the other side. The squirrel was full of the fear of death, the thrill of life. The squirrel was running across the street, how fun!

I considered going outside. I could run across the street and . . . I don't know. I could pick up the Starbuck's cup that had been tumbling down the street for the last couple hours, runover now, flat.

But I didn't. I picked the book up and started reading again. All that frivolous Algonquin witticism. I love it, but it *is* cloying. Even Dorothy Parker herself eventually had enough, and started writing political essays, anti-Nazi essays, essays in support of the Republicans fighting in the Spanish Civil War. She left a lot of her wit behind in favor of sincere political righteousness. And when she did, she fell out of fame. She faded and paled. No one wanted to read what she thought about politics. They wanted her to be witty, acerbic, scathing, frivolous. An Algonquin La Rochefoucauld. And she was a genius in that role. And pedestrian in the other.

Parker isn't the only writer to be undone by political sincerity. There are many examples. Gogol and Pound quickly come to mind. Pascal, even, with his desperate attempts to prove there is a Christian God. And Duras, too, whose political allegiances often detracted from her imaginative genius. Even if one agrees with Duras, as I mostly do, I don't go to her for political flag waving. Her artistic genius is too expansive to confine itself to myopias any Chomsky can achieve. Jane Jacobs' *The Death and Life of American Cities* is a great book and should, I think, be required reading for any city dweller in North America, but does it reach the heights of, say, Carson McCullers *The Heart is a Lonely Hunter*? Or Hugo's *Les Miserables*? No. It doesn't and can't. It's too straightforward. It's too mundane. It's perhaps not even fair to compare them . . .

But what about Baldwin? The speeches of Martin Luther King Jr? What about Zola or Dickens, Tolstoy? Do they succeed in addressing at one and the same time a specific political issue and that more personal (and more vague) nourishment of the entire mind and body?

I was thinking about this when I finished my coffee. The sky was light. It was day now, no one would argue that. It wasn't even early anymore.

My wife was still in bed. My daughter was still in bed.

I put the book down and walked out to the front stairs. The air was cold, damp. The sun was working hard to burn through the clouds, but the clouds refused to give in. Someone walked by with a black poodle on a leash. The dog shat in the neighbor's garden and I thought about saying something, but didn't. A jogger ran down the street in a blue track suit. A few crows looked down at me from the wire above. I should probably sweep the stairs, I thought.

After some minutes, I walked back in. The stairs would remain unswept. I went to the bedroom and crawled into bed with my wife.

The bed smelled something like death. Not like life at all. But what do I know, maybe that's what life smells like. Maybe not death, but something like an animal. And also something like burning tires. I was thinking about this, about the smell of animals, about life and death and how to live, how to really be alive, how to really be alive as much as you possibly can while you're here, alive. I was thinking about this when she rolled over against me. She touched me and I was smelling her life. Her body. She grabbed me then and I stopped thinking about whether I was alive or not, what to do and how, or why. I just felt her around me, moving against me, warm and wet and smelling like that.

And then it was over, and I fell asleep. I slept until noon and when I woke up the sun had won its struggle against the clouds. The sun had won, but I was not happy for it.

"Are you just going to lie in bed all day?" my wife said from the kitchen.

And she was right: morning was over. Day was half-finished and I had wasted it again. I would do little else. Nothing nearly as definitive as Jane Jacobs was able to do, or Noam Chomsky, or any of these people on Twitter with their short, declarative political opinions. I resolved, at least, to sweep the stairs, and this made me feel better, though I never actually got around to it.

POETRY GROUP

I am in a poetry group. A kind of book group, but we only read poems. I know, don't worry, this will be short.

This week our poem was Marianne Moore's "No Swan So Fine," about a swan sculpture—"at ease and tall"—from the Viking edition of her *Complete Poems*. That edition contains a Note on the Text that reads, "the text conforms as closely as is now possible to the author's final intentions." The author's final intentions . . . how is such a thing possible? I thought I would bring that up in our poetry group.

It also claims that "punctuation, hyphens, and line arrangements silently changed by the editor, proofreader, or typesetter have been restored," and that "misleading editorial amplifications of the notes have been removed." The Note on the Text is authored by Clive Driver, literary executor, and it's as seemingly punitive as it is brief. I thought I would bring that up, too, in our poetry group.

When it came time, I mentioned the severity of this Note, but no one seemed interested. No one *seemed* interested, I think, because no one *was* interested. This is a not uncommon response to the things I say in our poetry group.

We were sitting in the park. Behind the museum. The bugs were out. We were swatting them as we discussed, not the Note on the Text or even the poem, "No Swan So Fine"; we were instead discussing the unfortunate blind spots in the current political landscape. How the far Right sees only the far Left's intolerance, and not its own. And how the far Left sees only the far Right's intolerance, and not its own.

This conversation wasn't really going anywhere, so eventually someone opened the book and read the poem, and we fell silent. The poem had no concern for the materialism of politics, that much was evident. The poem was not interested in participating in any willing myopia or reductive thinking such as is required to think in political terms. The poem was performing the opposite act. Someone said, "the opposite gesture." The poem, "No Swan So Fine," wasn't even about a swan!

A stone, I suppose, in the shape of a swan. Kevin thought it was part of the fountain from the opening quote, from "the dead fountains of Versailles." But Allie said, "something like a candelabrum," referencing the Euphorbia tree appearing in the second stanza. Kathy said "china, it's china, you know, chintz china." And Sven just said, dumbly, "swan," merely recognizing the word but unable to follow its movement as it glided slowly through the poem, refusing to reveal itself as stone, statue, chintz china, or fall. I suppose it was a phantom.

"Perhaps it's all of these," said the one who had read it aloud, and we all groaned.

"What?" she asked.

"You can't just zoom out like that." said Allie.

"Why not?"

"I don't know . . . it's too cliché."

"Yeah, it's cliché," repeated Sven, the one who'd earlier said "swan."

"It's too vague," said Kevin, "we want answers!"

"Good luck with that."

"It's stone, okay. It's obviously stone. Or chintz china but who cares? You miss the point. It's not a fucking mystery novel . . ." Jordan said, with a little too much anger for a poetry group.

There was an awkward silence. I saw a child inside the museum put his face against the glass window, then his mother drag him away. I wondered who exactly Clive Driver was, and why he thought he had possession of Marianne Moore's "final intentions." Someone slapped a bug. A dog ran by, chasing a ball, then ran back with the ball in its mouth.

"Fucking Desantis," someone said, and then started talking again about the inability of the "human animal" to see its own flaws.

I asked which was the animal that could, but was unanimously ignored.

From a Dental Chair

"Reading's a waste of time," the dental hygienist said, hands in blue rubber gloves, blue rubber gloves in my mouth. I had been reading when she came in and she asked me what? I think I said something like, "oh it's a biography, but it's actually not a very good one."

"Yeah," she said, "I don't like to read much. I do like documentaries, though. I'm watching one now on the Challenger Space Craft. Remember that?"

"mmhmm."

"Open," she said, and filled my mouth with water. "Close." I closed, and the vacuum tube sucked all the water and saliva out of my mouth. "Open." she said, and the blue rubber gloves dove back in.

". . . a book, though, I don't know, sometimes when I'm reading a book I feel like my life is just passing me by. It's kind of a waste of time. Turn."

I turned.

"Good. I read one book recently about some farmers or something. I don't even know what was going on. They were on a machine, a tractor I guess. Turn your head to the side a little. Good. There were about eight of them on this tractor . . ."

"hmm."

". . . I know right. It was weird. Open. I think it was digging potatoes somehow, a potato harvester I guess, I don't know. Close."

I closed, and the vacuum did its thing again.

"It was the weirdest story. Open. There was a fight between two of the farmers. I guess farmers isn't the right word. They were like itinerant workers, I guess. Not Mexicans, though. Okay put your head straight again. They were white, I guess. Oh you're bleeding. Are you flossing?"

"mmm . . ."

"You really need to floss every night."

"umhmm."

"I love Mexican food, though. You like Mexican food?"

"mmm."

"My favorite are those fajitas. I think that's so fun the way they serve them on those iron skillets you know?"

"mmm."

"all sizzling there at the table, it's so fun . . . but margaritas are too sweet for me. My husband will drink two or three but I just have a Seven-up. If he has three I have to drive. Close. Good. How we doin?"

"Good."

"Good, now let's turn your head to the side a bit again, right there, almost done . . . He says tequila is his weakness . . . ha! tequila and any other alcohol. You know what I mean?"

"umhmm."

"But I guess we all have our weaknesses. Mine's documentaries. I could watch documentaries for hours. The History Channel. I love history. The one on the Challenger Space Shuttle was real good . . . you know they knew right?"

"hmm?"

"They knew. The O rings were . . . well they knew the O rings would fail."

She took her hands out of my mouth and I took a deep breath.

"Okay?" she asked.

"Yes." I took another deep breath and she threw her hands back into my mouth.

"I guess it was the engineers. They tried to tell the, the officials you know, of the, of the launch I guess, but they wouldn't believe them."

"hmm."

"Yeah, I wasn't clear exactly who knew what but they knew that the O rings would fail. Open wide now. Those poor astronauts."

"mmm."

"It's one of those things where you remember where you were, you know?"

"mmm."

"I was a freshman in high school. I didn't like high school very much. Okay let's rinse you out now . . . and close." She put the vacuum in and sucked out all the water. "Okay, almost done. Turn just a . . . perfect. I think they had it on in my Social Studies class, and everyone . . . I'm gonna have you close your mouth just a little bit. Right there. Great. Everyone just gasped like 'oh no!' "

"mmm."

"The way the spaceship just exploded out of nowhere . . ."

"mmm."

"Those poor astronauts."

"mmm."

"All those bits of burnt bodies all flying through space and sizzling, melted skin and faces and everything . . ."

"hmm."

"It must've been terrible."

"mmhmm."

"Just think of the expression on their faces when they knew they were about to burn to death."

"hm?"

"Close. Good . . . but books. I don't know. A book is too much to suffer through. I'd much rather watch something."

Reading Rilke (in a Sound Bath)

> "Fame—the aggregate of all the misunderstandings that collect around a new name."
>
> —Rainer Maria Rilke

I find it bizarre that the New Age community has embraced Rilke. Why? Why do they take his lines and place them around images of waterfalls and clouds, then package them as greeting cards or needlepoint wall hangings? I can't help but think that Rilke would be nauseated by most people who find him "inspirational." They've certainly never read an entire poem of his. And even if they have, you can't convince me that they've understood it. You can't convince me that they haven't just reduced it to whatever feel-good spiritual slogan they most recently heard in yoga class or while luxuriating in a sound bath.

Rilke would have us tear ourselves out of the social and religious clichés that to him were soporific. For Rilke, to be asleep was the ultimate crime. And what is a cliché if not a suspension of the mind? A hammock for thinking, or lack thereof? Rilke is a storm seducing storms.

Perhaps this misunderstanding is the fault of his patron, Princess Marie von Thurn und Taxis-Hohenboke. Or rather, not her fault but the fault of the fact that Rilke seems to be writing with one eye on flattering her, and one eye on his sense of isolation. You could read the entire *Duino Elegies* as an over-the-top, shamelessly ingratiating grant application. (You could, but you shouldn't.) It is this tone, I think, that those who frequent theosophy bookstores with names like Far West Pathways find so inspiring.

When he famously asks, in the *Elegies'* opening lines, "Who, if I cried out, would hear me among the angelic orders?" I'm guessing he didn't think it would be the folks at the Aspen Food Co-op, or the teacher of Thursday evening's Pilates and World Peace class.

His books are now face-out beside Thich Nhat Hanh, Chogyam Trungpa, and Bhagwan Shree Rajneesh in New Age bookstores all across the Western world. Here's a calendar with his quotes. Here's a yoga deck with fifty-two cards, fifty-two positions, fifty-two Rilkean reductions. And here's an embroidered pillow with "Many a star was waiting for your eyes only," written beneath the image of a child and mother gazing longingly at each other.

It's enough to give you food poisoning, this making mush of the minds of the Western World. Please, if you would, leave Rilke alone.

And lest we forget, in a letter to the Duchess Aurelia Gallarati-Scotti written in the 1920s, Rilke praised Mussolini and described fascism as a "healing agent." Fascism is a healing agent. Why have I never seen that on a pillow in Mystic Journey Books and Gems?

V.

LOVE AND SEX

*In which the author plays the role
of a mishappen Don Juan*

My Mouth: Ducks, Geese and Peafowls

If there's anything that marriage has taught me, it's that there's never really a good time to open my mouth.

I think it was Victoria, BC. We had a few hours before the ferry arrived, so we drove to a little park not far from the bay. It wasn't raining. And when it's not raining in Cascadia, the beauty can be so intense that it's hard to comprehend. The deep dark of the fir trees set off the dazzled blast of rhododendron flowers. Every camelia was a cornucopia of red and pink petals spilling to the ground beneath it.

We sat on a bench in the sun and watched some children feeding peacocks, ducks and geese. In a small pond a white swan glided, three ugly ducklings trailing behind. A raven gurgled high up in one of the cedar trees surrounding us.

She was the one who said it. That we had died and found ourselves in some sort of menagerie.

"... but then we would be inside, I guess," she said.

"Inside?" I said, confused.

"Menagerie comes from ménage, a household. If we were in a menagerie, we wouldn't be outside, in the park. We'd be inside, in a house."

"I see . . ." I said.

"Why do you say 'I see' like that?" she said.

"No reason ... isn't it related to manage?" I wondered, "That would mean there's a hand involved. Manage means hand, mano a mano. The hand that manages the *managerie*."

"But it's an 'e' not an 'a'," she corrected.

"I'm pretty sure it's an 'a'," I recorrected.

"No," she insisted, "it's the same as ménage a trois, a household for three."

"No," I said, annoyed, "it's like manage, manager. Think of a zookeeper."

"I won't think of a zookeeper," she said, annoyed. "A zookeeper has nothing to do with it."

"A zookeeper has everything to do with it! A zookeeper keeps the zoo, while a hand *manages* the birds in the *manag*erie."

"You can't spell, dear, and you never could. You know this about yourself." She said this with finality. "And besides, why do you insist on getting in these stupid arguments."

"It's not a stupid argument, you just have the word wrong. And I won my second-grade spelling bee for your information, which is how I got Kim Baldinger to go with me."

"To go with you where?"

"Nowhere. Just to date me."

"Where did you go on your date?"

"Nowhere? We might have gone to the zoo, once. But I doubt it. We were in second grade. We just said we were dating. Not dating but going together . . . But that's not the point. The point is that you're being illogical."

"This is absurd," she said.

"You're being stubborn," I said.

"Look it up," she said, and walked off.

"I don't need to look it up," I yelled after her. "*I know I'm right.*"

She didn't respond. She just kept walking. I sat still, refusing to go after her. Let her have her fit, I thought. The sun was out. A magnolia tree seemed almost liquid there were so many creamy flowers floating in it. Like a fountain. A peacock walked slowly closer to me, its blue and green iridescence like an ancient otherworldly glaze. It looked at me, a bit viciously for such a beautiful bird. I smiled, for some reason, and it stared expectantly, coming closer, glaring at me. When it realized

I wasn't going to give it any food, it looked at me as if I was the most useless thing it had ever seen. I stretched my hand out, as if there were something in it. The bird stepped forward, craned its neck, saw there was nothing in my hand, and looked like it wanted to kill me. Then it strutted slowly away.

The Flower Sellers of Rome

The flower sellers in Rome come in the form of wandering Bangladeshi men. Sometimes North African, but never the young London poor. Often they carry a bundle of red, long-stem roses. You might mistake them for romantics. You might mistake them for lunatics. (Is there a difference?) I suppose they are both. Romantics due to the fact they are living in Rome, and lunatics because, well, doesn't the moon pull all of us this way and that? These wandering flower sellers shipwrecked in Rome.

In actuality, they are something like enlightened monks. At least, that's how they present themselves. And they do present themselves! You cannot walk through the Borghese Gardens without encountering them. And, like any Don Juan, once encountered, consumed.

"Excuse me," they say, in any language you speak (they are professionals), "a rose for you?" And they hold a rose out for you. Your hand, despite your suspicions, reaches to take it.

"Please," they say, "for the lady . . . a gift."

Or:

"Please," they say, "for the child."

Or:

"Please," they say, "for your beautiful chihuahua . . ."

In a word, they will say anything. They will say anything so long as you take the rose. You must accept the gift. The rose, of course, is always a gift. It is always free.

"A gift," they persist, "for the lady . . ." (or child or chihuahua).

Try to walk away, I dare you. You can't. They will follow you, rose extended out to you, your wife becoming nervous.

"Sir, sir, please, a gift," they say, "It is a beautiful day!"

You must accept. And eventually you do. The man is a holy man, after all. Or something like it. A monk in the House of Love. And besides, his persistence is annoying. You take the rose so he will go away.

"Grazie," you say, "arrivederci," hoping he'll think you're a local, and not a tourist.

"Prego," he smiles, though he knows you don't really speak Italian. And for a second you think that's it. Perhaps you were wrong to judge him so harshly. Maybe it *is* just a gift. Maybe he *is* a monk in the House of Love. You should really be more trusting. I mean, you're in Rome! You're in Rome wandering through the Borghese Gardens! You're in Rome wandering through the Borghese Gardens with your wife, child, and chihuahua! Isn't it Romantic! The fountains and the umbrella pines. The waif playing accordion beside a statue of Pan. The rickshaws lined up outside the café. The water clock whistling in the distance. Smell of panini and cheap perfume, a single swan gliding past the columned pavilion on the banks of the little pond.

You look at the rose you're now holding, and sheepishly offer it to your wife. She smiles, confused. Not exactly swept away. The monk is lingering nearby, and then he returns. He was always hovering just a few paces back. He's a professional. He knows exactly how long to stay away: just long enough for you to think that the rose was a gift, and not a grift.

"Signore," he says, flattering you by speaking Italian. Of course, he doesn't speak Italian either. No one speaks Italian in Rome, in summer in Rome.

You turn. He's following you.

"Signore," he says, "for the rose?" He holds out a hand. He's thin, dark, beautiful in a saltimbanque sort of way. You wonder if he's not Bangladeshi after all. Maybe a romani. You've been warned about them. All the guidebooks conspire against them. "Beware the gypsies!"

You think to protest, "but you said it was a gift? Where went the monk? Where the House of Love?"

"Signore, per favore?" His eyes are deep. Full of longing. Longing tinged with the subtlest scent of mischief. He knows he has you. To refuse him now would somehow be inhumane. There are witnesses. Your wife has seen it all. And so too the child and the chihuahua.

"Signore, please?" He says again, his palms up, more roses in a canvas bag strapped around his shoulder. He could've been painted by Caravaggio, thin and sallow, a sick Bacchus.

"I thought it was a gift," you say, despite yourself. Despite how tacky it is to say it. Your wife grimaces. Why ruin the illusion? Just give him the money. Your daughter leans against you. The chihuahua whines.

"Per favore, Signore, cinque euro, please, sir?"

"Cinque!" you say before you think.

"Honey . . ." your wife says, in a mix of annoyance and anxiety.

You hand the man five euros. He smiles. "Grazie mille, signore." The monk is back. He's holy again. He even puts his hands together in a prayerful gesture of gratitude, and bows. He is a saint, a holy beggar, and he's blessed you. You've been made holy yourself, if also a fool.

Before he turns to leave, he says, in perfect English, "Enjoy your stay in Rome, my friend."

Postcard from Chapala

Some things just won't last. You think that if you write them they will. You think it's like magic, a spell. You think it's like Voodoo, that kind of writing. And it is, the way you do it. But it doesn't work. It never works. It never works the way you want it to. Something else happens. Something that is nice, but not exactly what you want.

I met her in Mexico. She had been there a week or more, in the little town on the lake. She was on a writing residency, and I went down to join her. I wasn't supposed to be there. No visitors were allowed. But I went anyway. She asked me to, and I did.

When I arrived, we devoured each other, and then lay in bed until we heard someone yelling, "frambuesas!" She put on a sarong and went to the door. She came back with a bag of raspberries. We ate them all, there in the bed, talking lazily about nothing in particular. We made love again. We were young. It was like that then.

That's all we did that day. That first day that I was in town. No writing happened that day. There were stains on the bed. At first we thought it was blood, but then realized it was the raspberries. When night fell, we fell with it. We didn't even eat dinner.

The next day a riot of bird chatter woke us up early. "Song" is hardly accurate. Cacophony isn't word enough for what it was. It was a disaster. It was a disaster of birdswear. The recycling trucks eating barrels of glass bottles along the cobblestone streets sounded almost lovely next to these birds. Fantastic. Apoplectic.

I made coffee on the stove. On a small terazza with a table and chairs, I wrote postcards to friends. I read D.H. Lawrence's *Mornings in Mexico* while she wrote at a desk inside. On the walls around the desk, she'd stuck little notes, quotes from other writers, to help get her through her project. Those little notes were the audience cheering her on.

I was the audience distracting her. I wasn't much help at all. She was wearing the sarong around her waist and nothing else. Her breasts were perfect. She was difficult to resist. I turned my chair so I wouldn't bother her. It was no use. We made love again, and then I left so she could get some work done.

Down by the lake, the malecón was empty. It was noon, and the locals only walked there at sunset. The heat grew exponentially as the sun stalled above the lake. The malecón had been recently redone, so the trees were small and gave little shade. The lake was dry, and shallow, and had receded a hundred feet from the high stone embankment. Someone had spray-painted "Chivas Manda!" in red paint on the wall. A flotsam of rowboats lay piled in the brown grass and bushes. Down by the water, a man in a straw hat wandered slowly behind two horses and a donkey grazing the shore.

I wound my way through the narrow streets, taking pictures of people's balconies, of old doors, of tiny Volkswagen bugs. I found a market and bought some cheese, avocados, oranges and limes. I bought a stack of fresh tortillas at a tortilleria, and then some tequila at a liquor store. A stray dog followed me for a couple blocks. I took a picture of it, too.

When I got back to our place, she was dressed, though still at her desk. I put the things away and made drinks. I set hers on her desk and took mine out to the terazza. A huge tree arched over it, filling the eastern half of the sky. The grackles chattered in the branches, but not as loud as they'd been that morning. A gas truck selling bottles of propane drove by with an obnoxious recording advertising its brand. I watered the plants, which no one seemed to be taking care of. There was a citrus tree, half-dead, in a ceramic pot. Some cacti. Aloe. A citronella, I think. All of it ill, wasted, withered.

I went inside to make myself another drink. She hadn't touched hers.

The sun refused to go down. I stared up into the trees. I was sweating just sitting there. The pale sky hazed over, and you could just make out the mountains on the other side of the lake, brown and barren and forbidding. She sat at her desk making notes in the margin of a book, I sipped my tequila, then took out a postcard and started writing. "Some things just won't last. You think that if you write them they will . . ."

TRAINS AND TEA HOUSES

We were in the subway. We'd been fighting. It was the three of us. (Liz is always saying triads are inherently unstable.)

Alli was fifteen at the time. The guy she'd met online (older by two years) drove in from New Jersey to see her. We were only in New York for a week. We had a lot to do and I found the attempted teen romance both ill-advised and annoying. There was nothing wrong with the guy, I guess. I suppose I just wasn't ready for this sort of thing. At least, I wasn't ready to witness it. Alli and I were barely speaking.

Liz and I weren't really speaking, either. We'd all been at her parents' for Thanksgiving, and something I'd said offended her. I thought it was nothing, certainly nothing worth fighting over.

"Why do you act so obnoxious at dinner parties?" she said.

"Why do you act so daft?" I countered.

"Daft?"

"Yeah, daft, daft and dumb . . ." there was a silence the New York City subway system has never known. ". . . not dumb, you're not dumb, of course. You're incredibly smart. That's the problem. You're incredibly intelligent but at dinner parties you act, well, kind of dumb on purpose. Demure and daft and docile. Why do you do that?"

The fight had started from nothing, but quickly escalated into something, and now everything seemed to be riding on it. How we would remember our entire trip.

Alli just stood there watching us. I could tell she was deriving no small amount of pleasure watching me dig myself deeper and deeper. Liz just glared.

So there we were, in the subway, the three of us. Waiting for our train. None of us speaking to the other. All of us wishing we'd never met the other. Never chanced into this or been born into this. All of us wishing we could just get on different trains.

I was staring into the dark grid of tracks and girders, I-beams, rails, posts and wires. A rat ran along one of the tracks. Someone was playing "Jingle Bells" on a baritone sax. Too soon, I thought. It's still

November! The trains kept blurring by on the express tracks, or crawl-ing by on the express tracks. The lighted windows in the cars illumi-nated the bored faces of passengers staring out or scrolling through their phones. I thought of something I read once, about trains and tea houses being the stuff of short stories and not of real life. I tried to re-member where I read it, but couldn't. I thought of asking Liz, but she wouldn't have responded. It would've just made her mad. Her back was to me. Maybe Chekhov, but it wasn't him who wrote it. Maybe someone wrote it in reference to his stories? Maybe that book Serge wrote about the painter Levitan, about Chekhov and Levitan's friend-ship. I don't know, I couldn't remember where I read it, but I liked the idea, even though it wasn't true.

We all just stood there. Each in our own stubborn quiet. Each hav-ing a horrible day. I wished I was in Moscow, or taking a train across Siberia, like Chekhov did. Siberia sounded nice right about now. An endless empty landscape, snow-covered, littered with little houses, alders. You could see across the tracks, through the darkness to the other platform. People standing there. Waiting for the train. And the express trains blurring by full of people, tired people, lifeless people. One of the trains slowed and then stopped on the other side, at the Uptown platform. The platform emptied onto the train. And the train onto the platform. The platform and train exchanged their emptiness. Everyone seemed to be in a trance, a kind of numbness. No one spoke. No one looked at anyone else. When I did see someone look out the window, they looked out the window at us, and they didn't seem too impressed. Not that we were, it was only the hatred in us that was impressive—but they wouldn't have seen that. They didn't care what they saw. They were dulled by the city, deadened by it. That was obvi-ous. Even I could see that.

"Should we go get some tea?" I asked, but no one replied, just the sound of Jingle Bells and the terrible clack and scream of an express train whining through the station.

Moonstone Brings Passion (to Other People Maybe)

We were on a kind of date, I guess. Well, we were on a date. That's exactly what we were on. Or she was. I guess I just wasn't into it. My marriage had only recently fallen apart, and I didn't have the emotional capacity for even the most casual relationship.

Carrie was a friend of a friend. She was a friend of my ex-wife's as a matter of fact. I'd met her a few times, when my wife and I were still together. She was funny, beautiful, intelligent, and successful in business (she ran a yoga studio). I was none of these. I liked her sense of humor, but I wasn't much interested in the rest. Not that it was her fault. I wasn't interested in anything at all following my divorce, certainly not in the first few months following my divorce.

It might've been my ex-wife who convinced me to go out with her. That sounds right. I considered it, but not seriously. It seemed offensive to me, and manipulative. She wanted me to move on. I wasn't ready for that. But when we ran into each other at the café, Carrie said hello. I said hello back.

It was she who asked me if I wanted to go to the lake for a picnic. Sure.

That weekend we found a patch of grass along the shore. One without goose shit. It was May. Not hot at all. Not even, really, warm. She wore a light coat and pants, sandals, some sort of blouse or button-down thing. I was in a state of disregard. I wasn't dressed to kill. I was dressed to be ignored. I think I had a hoody on.

On the drive there, our conversation was mostly forced. I picked her up. I had a cooler, a blanket, some salad, cheese, olives, and two bottles of wine. She had baked a loaf of sourdough bread. She bakes bread, too, for gods sakes, I remember thinking.

We couldn't have been more different. Carrie was an eternal optimist, interested in "self-betterment." My position has always been that the self doesn't exist (that is, a static self possessed by an individual who can shape or improve it). But if the self does exist, I would grant that it's only purpose is to self-destruct. My life up to that point had been a series of self-sabotages, while I could tell Carrie was a kind of Midas figure: everything she touched "was just lovely." The bread was delicious, of course.

"Isn't it just lovely?" she said.

"Yes."

"And the lake, the way the geese reflect as they fly over . . ." she said, as she opened a jar of vegetables she'd pickled herself. "Try this," she said, "and put an asparagus stalk into my mouth."

"Umm," I said, "very good."

"It's very easy. I can give you the recipe."

I didn't want the recipe.

Once we started drinking wine, things began to flow more smoothly. She'd been reading Virginia Woolf. I asked her if she thought Woolf had really put rocks in her coat when she walked into the river and drowned. She said she hadn't heard that. She said she didn't like to think about Woolf's suicide. It was too dark.

"Suicide tends to be dark."

"I guess so," she sighed.

"I read somewhere that she was walking her dog when she did it. Sometimes I think about the dog."

"Oh," she said.

"How the dog must've just watched her walk into the river and drift away. Maybe it thought she was playing some sort of game? Maybe it even swam along with her for a while. Or maybe just watched from the bank as she disappeared under the water . . . did it bark? Was it sad? That dog must've been so confused, standing there alone on the bank. What could it have been thinking as it watched her disappear under water? Something like, 'God these humans are so weird.'"

I laughed, she didn't. We were quiet for a while. We both sipped our wine.

"Still," I went on, despite the awkward silence, or because of it, "it's not as bad as Anne Sexton."

"Oh, I don't really know her. Isn't she a poet?"

"Was a poet, yes."

"Hmm," she said, "I've been thinking I should read more poetry. Maybe I should read her . . ."

"I wouldn't."

"Oh . . ."

"Well, *Live or Die* is worth reading, but by the time she publishes *The Awful Rowing Toward God* she sounds desperately insane . . ."

"The awful rowing toward God?"

"Her last book . . . before she killed herself."

"I like that title," she said, trying to keep the conversation light.

"It's the worst title I've ever heard," I thought, but didn't say it. I almost said it but decided my behavior was bad enough already without starting an argument. I smiled instead.

We were quiet again. We both sipped our wine. A willow nearby already had its leaves. The new, bright green leaves of spring. I remember thinking that I'd somehow missed spring that year. It was May but it was still cold. Perhaps it never came. Perhaps it wouldn't. Maybe it was my fault.

She had studied film in college. We talked a little bit about that, but whatever the topic of conversation, it soon ended. Nothing stuck. The silences between topics were confusing, and unfortunate. I think she was feeling it, too. The wine could only do so much.

We struggled through our catalogues of knowledge. More of a list than a conversation. The sun began to set. The few people who had been at the lake were gone. We were still lounging, the food sat on the blanket mostly uneaten. I had brought two bottles of wine. The white now finished, I opened the red.

"I don't usually drink," she said.

". . . in the morning?"

She laughed, confused. "No. I mean, yes. I mean I don't drink very much anytime. Two glasses are a lot for me."

It's true I'd drunk most of the first bottle.

"I'm sorry," I said weirdly, as I poured the red wine into a coffee cup with the image of Warhol's Campbell's Soup can stamped onto it. "I guess Marguerite Duras used to drink three liters of wine every day."

"Is that a lot?"

"Four bottles."

"Oh wow . . ." she raised her wine but didn't take a drink, "you might have to carry me back to the car," she forced a laugh.

I did the same. I kept trying to think of a way to end the night that wouldn't be too painfully awkward. A somewhat sickly moon was fighting its way through the clouds over the opposite bank.

". . . at least Duras didn't kill herself . . . I guess," I said, and sipped my wine. "They named a staircase after her."

She ignored me. After an awkward silence, she said, "Look, there's the moon."

I looked. There it was.

She put her hand on my leg. "They say moonstone can bring passion, balance, prophecy, and luck."

"Really?" It would be lucky to somehow get out of this, I thought, emptying my cup. I wasn't sure what to do with her hand, so I just left it there, on my leg.

"We use it in our classes to help people balance. Not only in the obvious, physical way, but emotionally and spiritually, too."

"Cool."

"Yeah . . . it's really quite lovely," she said, and pulled her hand away.

I think I sighed out loud, relieved that the hand had gone.

The clouds swallowed the moon, and the sky lost most of its color. Night was nearly night. We seemed to be the only ones still at the lake.

"Let's go skinny dipping!" she said, suddenly leaping up.

"What?"

"Let's go skinny dipping! It'll be fun," she took off her coat.

"It's a little cold," I said.

"Cold?" she was unbuttoning her shirt. "I've gone skinny dipping in January before."

"That would be even colder."

"Come on. It'll be fun." She took off her pants. She was now in her panties and bra.

I was still sitting on the blanket.

She put out her hand, as if to help me up.

"I don't know, Carrie. I don't think it's the best idea." I said, but instantly regretted it.

She looked confused. She was standing there in her underwear. She stretched both arms out. "Come on," she pleaded.

What the fuck is wrong with me? I thought, looking at this gorgeous woman basically begging me to get naked with her . . . "It's very cold," was all I could say.

"Really?" she dropped her arms. "Are you sure?"

I thought I caught her looking at herself, and then it suddenly felt like I was rejecting her body. I felt terrible.

"I would love to," I said, "are you kidding me? You're absolutely gorgeous . . . and funny, and smart, but I . . ."

"It's okay," she said, "I understand." She started putting her pants back on. I grabbed her shirt, stood up and awkwardly helped pull it over her shoulders. I did the same with her coat.

We were quiet. The moon was out again. I corked the bottle of wine and started packing up our things.

"Pretty shitty date, huh?" she said.

I looked at her. The moon was still low behind her, and threw a long line of glamor across the whole lake. "Yeah," I said, "I guess so."

"Oh well," she said, "it's not the worst I've ever been on."

"That's very nice of you to say," I said. She laughed. She was very pretty when she laughed. I laughed, too. The first genuine laugh of the night. She grabbed my hand then. I held it, and kept holding it as we walked back to the car.

Portrait of My Wife as Botticelli's Venus

She was teaching in Rome and we left for Elba for the weekend. Was that it? Or was it Ostia? I think it was Ostia. We'd taken the train for the day. It was the closest beach to Rome. I never thought I'd be in Rome, in Italy. When I was a child, I never thought I'd be anywhere but southern Indiana. Then, as a teenager in New Orleans, I thought I'd never leave. Jason and I would die on the streets of the French Quarter, or rot in Orleans Parish Prison. What would he have thought of Rome? Would we have gotten drunk in the Piazza Navona, singing folk songs beside Bernini's Fountain of Four Rivers? Or outside Keats' apartment on the Spanish Steps? Could we have slept on the Pincio Hill? Or would they have arrested us in a rowboat on the Giardino del Lago? I'd never find out.

It was a short walk from the train station to the beach. In Ostia, the closest beach to Rome. We paid ten euros for two lounge chairs and an umbrella. There were three of us. The three of us. My daughter and wife, the women I love.

If you've been to a European beach, you know that it was not private. Our lounge chairs were in a thick grid of others, a heavy sea of azure umbrellas, an azzurro harbor of bathers. The men around us smoked in their Speedos. That is, they smoked cigarettes while wearing Speedos. The women had magazines, and pedicures, and plastic fluted glasses. I guess they were cups.

We settled into our temporary lodgings, our loungings, and I went to the bar to get us drinks. At the bar some old men were drinking and watching a motorcycle race that was playing on three TVs. I ordered a bottle of cold white wine, and three Pellegrinos.

"Che numero?"

"Diciassette."

"Okay, solo un minuto. We bring to you."

"Grazie."

"Prego."

I started back, weaving through the cigarette smoke and nail polish. There were a lot of butt cheeks between the bar and our umbrella, and when I got back, I warned the ladies of the situation.

"I wanna see the butt cheeks," Alli said. She was 11, and getting more and more curious by the day about anything even remotely sexual.

"Umm . . . I would caution against it," I said, and gestured to a dimpled buttocks not far from us that was the hinge mechanism between a pair of stubby legs and a giant, meatball-shaped torso. The woman was in the process of ungracefully removing a skirt patterned with pink flamingos.

"Oh wow," Alli said.

"Indeed," I said . . . "Don't stare."

"You pointed it out!"

"But I didn't say to stare."

"Can we go swimming now?" she said, just as the Pellegrino arrived, and an ice bucket with a sweating bottle of pinot grigio.

"Yes, in a second . . . which way is the ocean anyway? I'm not sure we'll be able to find it."

From our vantage point, all we could see were hairy backs and azure umbrellas, magazines and towels in a haze of cigarette smoke. I poured Liz and me a glass of wine. I sipped mine.

Liz was reading a history of Rome. Alli was staring at a lifeguard with an enormous amount of hair on his chest. He was flirting with an English tourist wearing a thong and peach blossom top.

"What are you looking at?" I asked Alli.

"Is that a lifeguard?" she said.

"Yep. And I think his friend wants to take him home as a souvenir."

"He's so tan," she said, as if in an opium dream.

Liz laughed, "molto forte!"

"If you act like you're drowning, he might swim out and save you," I said to Alli.

"Shut up, Papa."

"Shall we?" I said, finishing my wine. Alli and I stood up and stripped down to our swimsuits. Liz stayed behind with her book. I had on surf shorts that went down to my knees. As I walked through the crowd of speedos and thongs, I felt grossly overdressed, though pleased to be so. Few others were as pale as me. The one's who were seemed to be English or German tourists. The rest were either Romans or tourists who had spent much more time on the beach than us. We were used to the hot, filthy streets of Rome. You didn't seek out the sun there. You avoided it.

Alli and I navigated through the masses and found the sea. Gentle waves. Shallow beach. We walked out fifty yards or so before we could swim. We swam.

Floating on my back, the sky was pale blue. I thought of Raphael, Michelangelo, Rilke. I wasn't sure why Rilke was part of it? At least, he wasn't a painter.

"Papa, are there sharks in the Mediterranean?"

"Tyrrhenian."

She was standing near me. It was only four feet deep, even though we were pretty far out.

"Well are there?"

"I don't think so. You don't come across any sharks in Greek or Roman mythology, do you?"

"No, but what about those creepy dolphins with the teeth?"

"Which ones are those?"

"In all the fountains . . ."

"I'm pretty sure those are extinct."

This seemed to mollify her, and she dove under and acted like she was one of the dolphins, splashing and arching and diving and generally getting water in my eyes and mouth. Rilke said that Rome made him "overwhelmingly sad at first, due to the lifeless, gloomy, museum-like atmosphere it exhales." He found the ancient ruins "overvalued, decayed, and disfigured." After being in Rome a few days, though, Rilke writes that the sadness wore off and "one recovers oneself, though still somewhat confused, and says to oneself: 'No, there is no more beauty here than elsewhere, and all these objects admired by the generations, restored and repaired by the hands of workmen, mean nothing, are nothing, and possess no heart and no value." And then, in a deliciously unsavory remark, Rilke concedes that "there is much that is beautiful here, since there is much that is beautiful just about anywhere . . ."

"Papa!" Alli yelled, and I stood up. She was looking back at the beach. A gust of wind was rattling the umbrellas, and magazines and napkins, food wrappers and empty plastic bottles were flying off of people's lounges. There was a huge dark cloud beyond the bar and it seemed to be galloping toward us. I noticed the temperature had dropped. I could just make out Liz, lost in a tempest of ass cheeks and garbage.

Alli and I watched the mayhem. Sand was getting into people's eyes, and they were running around shouting and screaming. Then the umbrellas, one by one, lifted up and sailed north along the beach, some of them tumbling, some of them rolling in a circle like a fallen top, and some of them lifting straight up like dandelion seeds or some Mary Poppins fantasy. The bathers were frantic, holding onto their magazines, their drinks and their towels.

"Papa, look!" she pointed at the lifeguard and his lover. The thong and peach blossom had leapt into the hirsute harbor of his arms, wrapping her legs around his hips. They were fiercely making out. They couldn't care less about the wind. Alli was in shock, staring, mouth open, eyes wide. "I wonder if making out with tourists is part of his training?" I said, when I heard a ripping sound, and the hunter green awning at the bar started lifting up, then lifted off and flew thirty feet into a snarl of orange bougainvillea tangled in a clump of palm trees beyond the bar. The old men were still sitting there, unconcerned by anything other than the motorcycles racing around on the screens.

I looked for Liz in the crowd. And found her. She was sitting up in her chair, pouring another glass from the bottle of wine. Gorgeous. Calm. Like that Botticelli painting. An overeager Zephyr blowing giant azure flowers, garbage all around her. She smiled and waved at us, and we waved back.

My Mouth: A Horrid Rotunda

She said it was a "rotunda," but I said "greenhouse." That's all it took for us to start fighting. This happened a lot. More than I'm comfortable admitting. Whatever that means? I hadn't yet learned to keep my mouth shut. These stupid fights. And what's more, every fight, no matter how it started or what it was about, dredged up the old accusations of unfeeling (me) and overreacting (her).

We were at the botanical gardens. The daphne and witch hazel were blooming. It was cold and the air was damp. It wasn't raining but everything was somehow wet.

I'll spare you the details of the fight. I wasn't in the mood then, and I'm not really now. She landed a few blows for which I'd proven defenseless, and I tried hard not to say something fatal. Something that would end our relationship. I knew I could if I wanted, I could be that cruel, and that self-destructive. But we were in New York, and still had three more days before we flew back.

"Conservatory," I said.

She didn't respond. In fact, she turned her back on me and walked away. I followed. She stopped every time she saw a sign: Black Locust, *Robinia pseudoacacia*; Loganberry, *Rubus ursinus*.

"Are you okay?" I asked.

She didn't respond. She moved further ahead, avoiding eye contact, looking instead at the signs: Hellebore, *Veratrum viride*; Silk Tree, *Albizia julibrissin*.

"Are we just not speaking now?"

No response.

"Look, darling!" I said, feigning excitement, "a Break-up Tree, Latin name *Boyfriendjust needslobotomy*."

She smiled then and the rain that wasn't rain started to become rain, so we went into the greenhouse conservatory rotunda where it was warm and humid but unfortunately lacked a café.

"Too bad there's not a café," I said.

"You always say that."

"Not when there's a café. What the hell is wrong with people? Do they not want to have glorious lives?"

"Is a café all that's needed to have a glorious life?"

"Basically, yes. It's not rocket science. Coffee, steamed milk, lively atmosphere, delightful conversation . . ."

"Maybe you should open a café?"

"Maybe you're right? I could call it Quarrels, and advertise it as a place where people can come to have their domestic disputes in a safe, welcoming environment (with lots of bad art on the walls)."

"Will you please just stop. Is it so difficult not to be sarcastic? Can we for once just have a normal conversation?"

"Fine," I said, ". . . it really is a beautiful rotunda. Even if rotunda is such a horrible word."

What Was Happening

I remember it was late August. Still summer but something, already, was in the air. It's difficult to explain. The nights were cool, and in the park a few trees, though not autumnal, were making a sort of shift. Especially the ones that had been stressed by the summer heat and drought. There wasn't any color in them yet, but you could see what was about to happen. You could sense it, and see it, even smell it. I can't explain it.

I too was in the park. The trees and I. I was waiting near the museum for her. I can't remember why or what we were doing, what we were about to do. We weren't going to the museum. I had no book to read or coffee to drink. I was just waiting. In the shade of a huge beech tree. It was afternoon and it was hot. It was hot, but as I said, something was different. I'm not sure what we were about to do, or even what we had just done. I was just sitting in the park.

I do remember it was late August. That I'm sure of. Late August and I was sitting in the shade of the beech tree. Waiting. Something was in the air. Something marvelous. Something I didn't quite understand fully, but I could feel it. Somehow. I was there for that. And for her. And I was just sitting there, quiet. Listening. Feeling what was happening. You could see it. Waiting there that day. I hope I remember that.

Sea of Helle

I'm not sure how she found out, but she knew. I could tell she knew about us: the other one and me. We were off-and-on and now everything was confused. How many times had we broken up?

We were naked. In bed. In our twenties, our early twenties. It was a long time ago. We lived sixty miles away from each other. She moved up to the city, while I stayed back to finish school. Our love affair was long, several years, and full of mishaps. We never seemed to get our timing right. A couple times we tried to end it, but we failed at that, too.

I'd driven up the night before. Late. This happened a lot. We'd be talking on the phone, and one of us would say, "I wish you were here, so I could touch you." And I would drive up the freeway to the city, speeding. Sometimes drunk. Always in love. Always in lust. There was something wonderful about that time, being so young and so mad with desire. And something terrible about it, too. I guess it's always better to read about that kind of thing. Hero and Leander, the frantic pitch of romantic fever. It sounds great until you're the one whose swimming across the Hellespont every night.

We were still in bed. It was morning. Raining. She just came out with it. Matter of fact. "So I guess you're sleeping with her now . . ."

She was like that. She was very direct and communicative. It was alarming.

She was also very much into thoughtfulness. Thoughtfulness as a concept, as a principle of living. She talked about it all the time. She valued thoughtfulness and consideration for others above all else. I admired her for this. Hers was a noble pursuit. She was a good person, something very foreign to me. Something I never felt comfortable with. I hadn't come from people like that. Most of my relationships up to that point were straight out of *Les Liaisons Dangereuses*.

"It's not what you think," I said.

"I think you're sleeping with her."

"Well . . . I wouldn't put it like that."

"I'm sure you wouldn't."

"But we aren't really together like that. You said so yourself."

"I know but that doesn't matter. If you loved me you wouldn't be with her."

"I do love you."

She didn't say anything.

"Okay," I said, "you must know that not everyone thinks the way you do. Some people are like bees buzzing. The buzzing has nothing to do with thoughtfulness, or consideration for others. Or even love. Those things don't factor in at all. They're just looking for flowers, looking to forage, to pollinate, to flit from flower to flower. It's not necessarily cruel. It's just a different way of being."

"But it doesn't make sense . . . and it *is* cruel. I don't understand people like that."

"I'm sorry."

She started crying then. I hated when she cried.

"Of course, you're right," I said, "your way is a better way. It's more civilized. It's a more enlightened way."

She stopped crying and I held her.

"The world is complex," I said, vaguely. "People are on different trips. They have different values. Some people can't see beyond their own desire. Some people don't even want to."

"Do you want to?"

I didn't say anything. I was in my twenties. My early twenties.

She touched me, and then rolled over with her back to me. She put me inside her and we moved slowly, barely at all. We were quiet for a while, just feeling each other. I told her I loved her. I meant it. She moaned. I whispered, "You're right. Of course, you're right."

She wasn't crying anymore, but there was something profoundly sad happening. You could feel it. It was raining. She pushed herself back against me. She trembled. The spasm moved through her entire body. "I love you," I said, "I love you so much."

She turned over, then, and looked me in the eye. "I went home with Scott after work."

My Mouth: Your Mother or Everyone

We were talking about how everyone seems suddenly so sensitive. We were driving to her mother's house. It was my first time meeting her mother. We'd been together a month or so. So far so good.

I said something thoughtless, I guess. Harmless, but thoughtless.

"Please don't say that when we get to my mom's."

"Oh right, we can't say that anymore either . . ."

"Correct," she said.

"Wait, or is it just your mother who objects to that?"

"No, it's everyone."

"I think they changed it back, though. Now you can say it. It was changed but now it's come full circle. It's fine . . . in certain contexts, I think."

"My mother's house isn't one of those contexts . . ."

"Ahh, I see. Got it."

"Good."

"It's odd, though, isn't it? How it depends on whether or not you're up to date on the latest . . . the latest way to say things. Like the sentiment behind what you say is less important than the words you use to say it."

"I guess."

"In some ways, I suppose, it's a triumph of language. The basket becomes more important than its contents. The cart goes before the horse."

"Or the basket is both basket *and* contents," she said, "and the cart is both cart *and* horse. Meaning is in both. We communicate by what we say and how we say it. I don't think that's a new idea."

"No. I guess not."

"It's the same with clothes. Clothes are an indicator of the kind of person wearing them. So the words you use are indicators of the type of person you are."

"Hm . . ."

"So please don't use that word around my mother."

153

"Got it . . . I do think they switched it back, though. I think it's okay now . . . in certain contexts."

". . . in certain contexts?"

". . . with the best intentions."

". . . with the best intentions?"

"In certain contexts with the best intentions."

"Okay," she said, "but aren't intentions themselves a kind of context . . . even the best intentions?"

"I don't know."

"Anyway, just don't say it around my mom."

"Got it."

"And maybe just don't say it at all."

". . ."

"To be safe."

". . ."

"Agreed?"

"Sure."

The road curved quietly through a wood of oak and alder, and we curved quietly with it. It wasn't cold, but it looked cold. I was driving. There was a mist. I cracked the window. I get claustrophobic in the car.

"Actually, I think I disagree," I said, after some time.

"You disagree?"

"Yes, I disagree."

"How do you think we should say it, then?"

"I think either way is fine, in fact any way is fine, in certain contexts (around your mother not being one of those contexts, of course), and with the best intentions . . . so yes, I guess I disagree."

"What exactly are you disagreeing with?" she asked. I rolled the window back up.

"That good intentions are contextual."

"Okay?"

"Think of it. What if I say to you, 'oh look at you, you fat little dumpling you,' and mean nothing but the best. I mean only that you're cute and I love you, I love to see your cuteness. I'm overwhelmed by it.

I'm delighted by it, like you would be by a delicious fat little dumpling. That you're so cute that I want to just eat you up. Now, if I say that, you might be offended no matter my intentions, even if my intentions were (and they would be!) the best. The fat little dumpling is the content, but the context (my intentions) is subjective and therefore not really a context at all . . . right? They're just *my* intentions. Mine and mine alone. It's the same with art. It doesn't really matter what an artist's intentions are if they've written something, or painted something that someone finds offensive. Once someone gets offended they couldn't care less what the artist's intentions were. It's not fair, and I don't agree with it, but that's just the way it is. Don't you think?"

She didn't answer. We drove in silence. The mist glommed through the tops of the trees, I turned on the wipers, but the windshield wasn't wet enough so they chattered across in a harsh objection. I turned them off.

She was conspicuously quiet.

"What's wrong?" I said.

"Nothing."

It was obvious she was lying. "Are you sure?"

"That wasn't very nice."

"Are you kidding me?"

"No."

"Really?"

"It's fine. Forget it."

"I was just making an example."

"Yes but you know I'm trying to lose weight and that was very insensitive."

"Oh jeezus."

"You know you really say some terrible things."

"I'm sorry."

"It's fine but when we get to mom's don't be a dick, okay?"

"Fine."

Portrait of My Wife In Absentia

We were in Chapala, talking about D.H. Lawrence. I was reading him, too. We found the hotel where he and Frida stayed, before the lake dried up. When it was full and lapping against their front porch. That was before the construction of the malecón, which runs along the beach as a massive concrete barrier, so that the hotel feels remote. A block away. Not on the lake at all. Not like it used to be. When Lawrence was here.

For five weeks we stayed there, in that small town. We watched horses graze, listened to the grackles every morning, walked along the malecón where a little boy named Edgar asked Liz for a peso every evening, and every evening she gave him one. We saw him once in town, drinking milk from a plastic bottle.

"You're supplying his habit," I said.

"I guess so."

We went to the city a few times. To Guadalajara. To visit friends and tour the cathedrals. The porous stones the Spanish used to build them. They were haunted. We touched them. We drank coffee in the squares, noticing the men who shined shoes. How they didn't use rags. How they just used their hands, and how black those hands were with polish.

In June we went to the coast. Tourist season was over, and we found a cheap place in a small town north of Puerto Vallarta. The bus from Guadalajara nearly made us sick. We couldn't decide which was worse: the winding roads, the frigid air conditioning, or the action movie dubbed into Spanish, starring The Rock, we were forced to watch at a volume you could probably hear in Guatemala.

After several hours of traveling, we arrived on the coast. It was hot. Much hotter than Guadalajara, which was already hotter than Chapala. I had directions but they were no use, as most of the streets weren't marked. We wandered around for a good half-hour before we decided to ask for directions. A woman selling tortillas told us the way to Calle Santiago by pointing to a hill some distance behind her stand,

"Es allí." We climbed, on foot, with our backpacks and a suitcase Liz rolled, or rather dragged, over the streets made of cobble, gravel, and mud.

By the time we reached our place, we were sweating. I was drenched. We found the key, hidden for us by the owners, and let ourselves in.

"Should we drink the water?" Liz said, as I filled a glass of water from the tap.

"It's either die of dehydration or die of giardia," I said, and downed the glass in one gulp, then filled it again. "I mean, we've been in Mexico for five weeks. I think our stomachs can handle it . . . right?"

"I guess you'll find out," she said, putting her stuff down and crawling onto the bed.

"Let's go for a swim," I said, and started searching for my trunks.

"Oh god," Liz said, "I can't walk anymore." She took her clothes off and stretched out naked on the bed. "It's so hot."

I turned the ceiling fan on, but could only get it to spin slowly, as if the air was too thick for the fan to move through it.

Liz was lying on her back, her legs spread, her eyes closed.

"Are you okay?"

She let out a very quiet but nevertheless audible moan, something like an animal dying.

"I'll see if there's another fan." In a closet off the kitchen, some ants were piled around a sticky spot on the floor. On one of the shelves there was a small plastic fan.

"Here," I said, and plugged it in. I directed it toward her. She shifted on the bed so that the fan blew right between her legs. "It's probably cooler on the beach . . ."

She moaned again, "it's so hot."

"Let's go for a swim. You'll feel better then."

She didn't move. Her legs still spread. The fan blowing between them.

I touched her. "You're sweating." She moaned again. I put my mouth on her. Kissed her. She was salty with sweat.

"It's too hot," she moaned. "I have to sleep."

I stood beside the bed and watched her. She didn't move. Her nakedness spread across the bed. Her arms raised. She pulled her hair up so that it wasn't touching her shoulders.

"You look Greek," I said, "when your hair's like that."

She didn't respond.

"I'm going to find the beach . . . I'll lock the door."

The beach was only five or six blocks away. A thin strip of blond sand that followed the line of a wide, curving bay. Nearly a semi-circle, so that across the bay was a headland with a few houses mixed into the jungle. What seemed like a jungle anyway.

There weren't many people on the beach. I noticed some restaurants further down, or maybe a hotel. A few beach umbrellas clustered together. But here, where I sat in the shade of a fig tree, there was no one. A dog ran up to me, stared a second, then ran off.

I took my shirt off, then my sandals, set my wallet down and waded into the water. The sea was warm. The waves gentle. There was no rip to speak of. I swam out past the break and floated on my back. I thought of Liz's body, naked on the bed. The sweat beading on her skin, and the way her breasts fell heavy to her sides. I thought of the bus ride. How loud it had been. Why do people make themselves so miserable?

It's hard to imagine Lawrence swimming. Even in Mexico he was always wearing a suit and tie. That beard must've been intolerable.

After a while I started to feel like I was getting burnt. I swam back in to be safe, and sat in the shade for a few minutes. When I was dry, I made my way down the beach toward the umbrellas. The dog found me again. It followed me for a while down the beach. It didn't seem to belong to anyone.

People were selling sarongs on the beach, jewelry, shrimp, beer. I bought a beer and chatted with the guy who sold it to me, while he sprinkled chili powder on a lime wedge, and then fixed it to the top of the bottle. I carried my beer down the beach, and then walked between a couple of restaurants and into town. The town was small. Very small, but it did have a plaza. A plaza and a gazebo. A little girl was riding a tricycle around the gazebo. A few stray dogs lounged in the shade of a gnarled bottlebrush tree. My dog was there, too. I said hello but it didn't register. The girl on the tricycle stared at me blankly. I smiled. She rode away.

I found a small fruit stand and bought some limes, an orange, and a few avocados. Across the street was a liquor store. I bought a bottle of tequila and a bag of ice and headed back to our rooms.

Liz was still on the bed. Still naked. Still spread out like a Greek goddess. She didn't move. A Greek statue then. I put the groceries on the counter and walked over to her.

"Bueno Bueno?" I whispered.

Nothing.

"Buenos tardes, greca bonita . . ." I walked over and grabbed an ice cube. I placed it on her stomach. She twitched once, and then just lay there as it quickly melted in her belly button, then flowed down her side. I rubbed the cool water around her stomach, then grabbed another cube and rubbed it around her breasts, circling her nipples. Then another one over her pubic hair, one on her thighs, another down her legs.

Slowly she revived, and turned over. An ice cube in the small of her back, across her shoulders, up the back of her legs. She moaned.

"You're alive," I said, as she moaned again. The bed was getting damp. "The rest of the ice is for our drinks."

Down the hill someone was listening to music, but it was far enough away that the tuba and horns were the only instruments you could hear. Tequila, ice, slices of lime and orange. Liz rolled over when I brought her the drink. She propped herself up with some pillows, still naked. She looked exhausted, though she hadn't really done anything. The ceiling fan was spinning faster now. She sipped her drink and seemed to revive. Some dogs barked in the hills behind our flat.

"There are a lot of dogs in this town," I said.

She sipped her drink again.

It was hot in the room, but the drinks were cold and numbing. I wondered if Lawrence drank tequila when he was here. Or was he so devoted to temperance?

"Better a drunk than a teetotaler," I said, and clinked Liz's glass. She didn't respond.

I was in love with Mexico, with the heat and the sea and the birds and the dogs. All the filth, the dust and crumbling buildings, the way mezcal fills your mouth with smoke. Bougainvillea and mangos, papayas and parrots. The colorful masks and pottery, dresses and skirts hanging along the roadways outside of town. The old men on plastic lawn chairs, smoking in the shade of a breadfruit tree. There was no better place under the sun.

"I could never live here," Liz said. "It's insufferable."

VI.

Daniil Kharms
Made Me Do It

In which the author becomes increasingly more absurd,
despite the advice of all those around him

A Brief Supplication

Forgive me, Flynn Mcdaniel, for shaving half your eyebrow off when you passed out on the couch at Jenni Warner's party.

And forgive me, Willie Motts, for all the dents in your mother's wall (the errant pool balls were vaguely intentional).

And Steven Forester, I'm sorry I sold you three sheets of Sunday Morning Funny Papers we both hoped were acid (I assure you that I, too, lost a small fortune on that ill-fated southern Indiana drug deal cum paper route).

And Jonathon Avery, you should've listened to the football coach when he told you in no uncertain terms to avoid me at all costs, "that kid is nothing but trouble." And Coach Schultgeiss, I'm sorry I left a bag of dogshit wedged beneath your office door after I heard you turned Jonathon Avery against me.

And to my high school basketball coach, fuck you and all your imprecations, and for haunting my dreams the last forty years, even though the stakes were so very low and I was so very high (I'm sorry I was so often so very high).

Forgive me Blondie, Pat Benatar, for cutting the pictures out of the jackets of your albums and taping them to the wall beside my bed. To your icons I offered up so many unsavory thoughts. I, for one, do not share the hope that walls could speak.

And to Mary Brien, forgive me, thank you (!) for taking charge when I was as lost at sea as any teenage Odysseus, despite being in the backseat of the 1976 Pontiac Lemans passed down from sibling to sibling, where my sisters before me had, I presume, also grabbed hold of budding argonauts.

Forgive me, my sisters, for presuming such things.

Forgive me, all who knew me, as I struggled to scour myself of the foul culture from which I'd sprung. Forgive me what I've done and said. Forgive me, too, for what I cannot say.

And oh yes, Ms. Ong, surely dead now, forgive me for mooning you in front of the entire 7th grade English class—no teacher of public schools deserves such a rotten apple.

And Principal Edwards, forgive me for crying those three days of in-school suspension, alone at a desk in a room with the lights out, my father's belt marks still red on my back and ass.

And forgive me, father, for thinking only of washing my hands of that shitty world you offered me, as one might be offered a scratch card lotto ticket half-scratched already, painfully obvious there's no chance of cashing out.

The Fog Sat Down

I was reading Joan Didion's essay on water, on water in Southern California, when I noticed the fog outside was gone. Gone or changed. It had disappeared. The fog sat down on the pavement and turned to wet. Can something turn to wet and not be wet? Become something else? Move from noun to adjective? From fog (in this case) to damp. ("Of bodies changed to other forms I tell.")

I suppose it morphed. It condensed, the fog, changed from something more vaporous to something wholly liquid. And then, lacking sufficient architecture, sufficient scaffolding to sustain itself aloft, dropped while I wasn't looking, while I was looking elsewhere, looking in fact at an essay about the water situation (not good) in Southern California circa mid-1970s. That situation being presented in a pseudo-poetic journalistic mode characteristic of Joan Didion. A mode at once revolutionary for its time and typical of it. Impressionistic. Personal. Gonzo. It was, as Tom Wolfe called it, "The New Journalism." I remember thinking, confused by what the fog was doing, that bringing the personal into journalism was both exciting and a huge mistake.

When I shifted my gaze from elsewhere (1970s Southern California) back to where I was (in physical time and space), the fog was gone. The pavement was wet. The morning sky was not yet light. For some minutes I could only think (despite the water issues in 1970s Southern California) how delightful the world can be. How quietly lovely and harmonious in its material logic, its physical phenomena: wind and cold and humidity, barometric pressure, seasonal shifts, vaporization, condensation, angles of sun, moon, etc. all the things that occur while I'm not looking, that occur all around me always, affecting me even though I can't (or don't) see or know or notice and rarely (if ever) celebrate.

I resolved (again) to celebrate. And to let go of any idea I had that I had any idea about what was going on around me.

You're Never Too Young to Have Dementia

"You should write about it."

"What?"

"I just think it's so crazy."

"Oh, that . . . yeah."

"It would be easy to do."

We were in the kitchen. She was sitting at the bar. We called it the bar, but it was just a high table one of our neighbors left on the street after they moved out. We dragged it upstairs and into our apartment. She didn't want it at first, but then we started calling it the bar and now we use it all the time.

I set a gin and soda in front of her. On the bar.

"You never see things like that anymore," she said.

"No. It's true."

"Not here anyway."

"Not anywhere."

"Not anymore. It's extraordinary," she said, and sipped her drink.

I got up and pulled the bottle out of the freezer. The kitchen was small. The apartment was small. Not New York small, but small. The kitchen was very small. The fridge was just right there by the bar, and on the other side of it was the stove. I stood up, turned, opened the freezer, pulled out the bottle, turned again, and poured some gin in my glass. I left the bottle on the table. She poured me a splash of soda from the can that was already out.

"That's plenty."

"Sorry."

"It's okay. I can't believe I forgot the limes," I said.

"Ella's friend has dementia."

"I don't have dementia," I said. "And besides, Ella's friend is old."

"She's in her sixties."

"Well, that's old."

"Not to get dementia."

"No. I guess you're right. It's young to get dementia."

"You forgot the limes last time, too."

"Very funny . . ."

"Well you did," she said, and raised her eyebrows.

"I've always forgotten things. I used to go to school without my backpack all the time. My mother would have to drop it off for me."

"That's different."

"Can we change the subject? Want another drink?"

"Not yet," she said. "Ella said her friend will be eating dinner and then, five minutes later, ask when it will be time for dinner. And she'll actually eat a whole second plate of food. Ella says she's getting ... well, she's gained a lot of weight."

"Weird."

"She said zaftig."

"She said zaftig what?"

"Zaftig like her friend is getting zaftig."

"Zaftig. What is that? Hebrew?"

"Yiddish."

"Yiddish."

"Yiddish, it means fat. Not fat, really. More like plump. Full-figured."

"Uh huh," I said, and stood up, turned, grabbed some ice out of the freezer and put it in my glass. I turned again and sat down, filled my glass. She picked up the soda can . . . "No thanks," I said.

"I'll have one more, I guess."

I poured the gin from the bottle on the table into her glass, then stood up. "Where are the limes?" I said, looking in the fridge.

"Funny," she said.

I sat back down at the bar. The sun was coming in through the window. It was hot. The cold gin and sodas were a relief. They were perfect. I was trying to remember when she moved into this place. It had already been a few years.

"Do you think I'm zaftig?" she said, and stood up so I could see her hips.

"No," I said, "you're fat."

She hit my shoulder. "Anyway, you should write about it. It would be easy."

"Why don't *you* write about it?" I said.

"Maybe I will . . . you never see things like that anymore."

"No, it's true . . . you don't. But what if they find out?"

"Just change their names," I said.

"They'll know."

"Change the disease, then, or say she didn't kill herself. Say she went to Mexico . . ."

"Mexico?"

"Why not? On a writing retreat. Like Lawrence and Frida."

"I think you should write it," she said. "You never see things like that anymore."

"Yeah, I don't know . . . I can't believe I forgot the limes."

"You forgot them last time, too."

No Shoes Are Better Than Four

I never liked clothes. I'm no nudist, but I never liked clothes. I wear them of course, but I would be happy not to. Or to wear the bare min-imum (bare being the operative word). I could live where it's warm, and wear only swimmers, at most a loose shirt or linen slacks at night. Never socks. I hate socks. Socks feel like little straight jackets for your feet. The worst part of my day is putting on socks, and I leave it till the last possible minute, and take them off as soon as I can. Sometimes I take them off on my way home from work. I drive barefoot.

At the same time, I feel naked without a hat. I don't pretend to un-derstand myself. Socrates posed an impossible demand, and perhaps was a fool, when he spoke the words "Man, know thyself."

The times I've lived where it's warm have been, if I'm honest, the most healthy and contented days of my life. Even Taiwan, where the air was full of dust and lead and carbon monoxide, the fact that socks were not necessary made up for the sinus infections, the thick yellow mucus, the burning eyes and the potential for lung cancer.

In Mexico, too, socks are unnecessary. What's the point? Sure, peo-ple get dressed up there (as they do in Taiwan) but there's no need to. You can just sit on the terraza and listen to the parrots, the mariachi, or the men shouting "*elote!*" in the street.

I went a whole year without wearing socks in Australia. It was de-lightful. I nearly floated away. Socks are a burden, an anchor. They are the chains that Zeus used to bind Prometheus to the stone where vultures could pick out his eyes. What fool invented them? What pre-tentious, Edwardian fool said "oh how desperately we need some cloth to adorn the area above the shoe and beneath the hem."

Etymologically speaking, a sock is actually a shoe, and therefore unnecessary. What madman would wear two pairs of shoes? From Old English, *socc*, "a kind of light shoe," derived from Greek, *sukkhos*, "a Phrygian shoe." Phrygia is where Turkey is now, a desert country, on the Mediterranean. A place where you don't need socks! I don't blame the Phrygians for wearing shoes, especially "light shoes," but what dumbass, from what country, decided "these shoes work better if you wear another shoe on top of them?"

Going for a Walk to the Park on the Couch

We were sitting on the couch. She wanted to go for a walk, to the park. She was five or six, my daughter. I was her father, and very tired from a dinner party the night before.

"What if we just say the things we'd see on our walk?" I said.

"Like what?" she said.

"Well, you know, like the gardenia we smell on the stairs . . ."

"By the lavender!" she shouted.

"Yes, and the spit bugs that make those little gobs on the rosemary."

"Can we find one?" she said.

"Sure. Let's grab one."

We put our fingers out as if we were pinching a gob of spit, and rolled them until the spit bug came out.

"I got it," she shouted.

"Me, too," I said

"Let's keep walking," she said.

And we did keep walking, on the couch. We walked down the street past Diane's, who died one night and was carried out on a stretcher by several men in blue uniforms. And then walked across the street, past the fire hydrant that looks like a clown ("Hello little clown," she said). We smelled the roses on the corner. And found the statue of the alligator submerged in the lawn ("Watch out for its teeth!"). We stood under the elm tree while the seeds fell, and stayed there until we caught one. We walked all the way to the park to sit by the reservoir and watch the buffleheads dive and reappear. She told me a joke I'd heard a hundred times. I laughed.

"Ready to go back?" I said.

"Can we go to the swings?" she said.

"Sure."

And we did. We walked to the swings, on the couch, where I pushed her again and again, higher and higher, not really thinking that time would ever end.

After Ryokan; Portrait of the City I Live In

On the way to the market, you walk along the crowded streets. Hemmed in by boarded up storefronts, the smell of urine and spilled beer rises each time you pass an alley. Vomit. Feces. Men and women bent over like contortionists or centaurs, deep in the quicksand of a fentanyl high. The city unable to hold its citizens with grace. The city bursting. Not like a flower or fountain, but like a sore.

Seeking some harmony, you have come here. To walk. To walk anywhere. To get away from your screen. To walk outside is a great victory over the forces of inertia, sloth, and lethargy.

A blue tarp covers someone lying in the doorway of what used to be a Greek tavern. You won't know if the person is alive or dead. You won't check. There are too many. And besides, what would you do?

Sirens fill the morose winter air. There's little difference here between the living and the dead. After all, we all know the living will all soon be dead. And memories of the dead soon disappear. It's no secret. The only mystery of life is that it's gone on this long.

What is this room?

Nothing but misery scattered on the sidewalks. Feeling at home, you wander through, recognizing several scenes from several famous books. The stories are everywhere: you can't tell them fast enough, or well enough.

Later, walking back—your bag full of cheese, fish, wine—evening dims. You see that the lights in the buildings downtown have come on. The janitors are busy cleaning all night. The lit buildings cast shadows across a darkness light will never reach. A darkness that will only grow darker, and one day end.

EMPTY, VOID, HOLE OR PIT?

It makes little sense why life should be so painful. Until you consider gravity's constant, unrelenting pressure. Then it makes perfect sense. Gravity is the supreme oppression. I think this is why it's so easy for us to feel like victims. Because we are. We are victims of physics. All of us. How could we not be, in such a world? In such a physical world.

I do wonder if certain specific political upheavals are at their foundations more about a vague sense of oppression, a gravitational oppression and general discontent. If we are bound to inertia, we are also primed for riotous acts. There's always time to add the specific peculiarities of revolt later. How easy it is to rally others with slogans asking for change when all of us are trapped by the laws of physics. I'm surprised there aren't more October Revolutions. It's a great irony that discontent leads both to sloth and insurrection.

In this I think I'm aligned with Pascal, who knew well the forces of gravity. The immensity of forces beyond our control. I can't relate to those who walk around without that huge black boot weighing on their necks. Space is not the right word. Nor infinity. Not nothingness, void, hole, or pit. Not nihilism, pessimism, Cioranism, or any other ism. All our shuffled lexicon's unable to describe it.

Perhaps I'm being too linguistic. For some people language is only a tool with which to buy beans or bread at the market. But for those of us concerned with affecting a sense of wonder—that is, for those of us concerned with art—language is a midden of empty shells left after our attempts to cast spells that would trick a moment into lasting forever.

I suppose you could also just go swimming. Escape, awhile, gravitational pressure. After all, what need is there for revolution, or writing, when the water's fine and the breeze is right? I'm guessing no one ever stormed a castle who knew how to surf.

Cancún, Michigan

Our middle school science teacher was perpetually drunk. His slur was constant, and often led, like a medley, into some other sentence related purely by association (*his* association, not ours). His speech was so tangential only a lost sailor at sea could hope to understand it. It was a drunken patois few of us spoke . . . at least not yet.

My father used to give us beer when we were kids. Miller Light from a can. (In Milwaukee, you would never drink a beer that wasn't brewed in Milwaukee.) Just a sip, but I still remember the first time, the sour bitterness as the bubbles raced down my throat and up my nose. Some of the adults at the Jaycees spoke a similar patois as our science teacher. It may as well have been a foreign language. But because I'd overheard so much of it growing up—in bowling alleys, at softball games, bratwurst cookouts and summer beer gardens (my people, round and drunken!)—I found it weirdly soothing. I loved my teacher.

"Boys and girls please take out your books, if you didn't forget your books, your science books I mean of course, not any *Gatsby* or *Gargantua and Pantagruel*, not that you scholars would ever read such a thing as that, as the great literature of yesteryear . . ."

The class took out their books and mostly ignored the rest of what he was saying.

". . . and turn to page 169, aka, thirteen squared, aka *cent soixente-neuf*, aka does anyone here speak French? Lilith? You do? *Tres bien, Lilit! Vous voudrai chanter une petite chanson, Lilit?*"

Lilith looked confused.

"*Peut etre, 'Je Ne Regrette Pas'? La lala lala la lalala!*" he sang. The class just stared. I smiled, admiring the madness. "For extra credit, who knows the name of the French chanteuse otherwise known as the little sparrow? Not to be confused with *Little Birds*, which is not to be mentioned in a middle school classroom. Anyone? Anyone? Beuller? Anyone? . . . Okay class, grab the wrist of the person sitting next to you and feel for a pulse . . . is anyone alive in here? Am I the only one!"

I loved to watch him sweat, the way he pitted-out his shirts, his verbal wander, how he blathered. We didn't learn much science. I learned a lot about the English language and how malleable it can be, but very little beyond Hydrogen and Helium in the Periodic Table.

Sometime while I was in high school, he died. His daughter was a grade above me, and she missed school for a whole week. She went with her family to Cancún, where they threw his ashes in the ocean. We were all jealous. We all hoped that our fathers would die before we graduated from school, so we could have a week off, so we could go to Cancún.

The night I heard about it, I asked my dad where he wanted his ashes strewn. But he didn't say Cancún. He said Michigan.

A Note On Revision

Writers have strong opinions about revision. Some love it, some hate it. Some think a work only gets worse by revising, some that it only gets better. The "raw vs. the cooked" has been cooked to death.

For me, I find my work generally gets more intelligent as I revise. Not that the writing necessarily gets better. It's just that the things that I'm saying grow more thoughtful the more I consider them, the more I go over them. Sometimes this self-reflection allows me to think better of including this or that nasty remark. So I edit it out. Sometimes not. Sometimes I miss a few things.

I do reach a certain point, though, where the revision process has to end. This is because, as the work gains in thoughtfulness and consideration, so too does the notion that I probably shouldn't publish it. That, for those few unfortunate souls who will read it, it will only cause offense, suffering and regret. So, as my manuscript becomes more intelligent with every revision, I eventually reach a point where I think to myself, "you know, you probably shouldn't publish this. You'll only make enemies. Maybe just go for a walk instead."

A CHRISTMAS CAROL

"You should write something about Christmas," my daughter said. She loves Christmas.

Me? I don't really understand it, I guess. I'd rather not write about it, or any other holiday for that matter. But Christmas especially. I suppose that's the special thing about Christmas. It's the most abhorrent of the holidays.

To be clear, I don't have a problem with Christ. He seems wise enough. Benevolent, righteous, eternal, etc., all the things you would expect to find in the son of God. It's the Christmas-goers who are the problem for me. No offense to my daughter. Whom I love.

By Christmas-goers I guess I mean all the people who go about celebrating Christmas. The insincerity is too much for me. All that maudlin tripe and tacky well-wishing (to say nothing of the insatiable consumption, poor color scheme, and inflatable Nativity scenes).

"Merry Christmas," they say. What does that even mean? "Happy New Year," on the other hand, makes sense to me: a wish for happiness throughout the new year. But Merry Christmas? What is that? It's a bit trivial, isn't it? A wish for merriment on Christmas day? One day. Have a great day. That's it? Okay, wow, thanks for your well-wishes. You have a great day, too.

"Great" isn't even accurate. The Christmas-goers insist on "merry." Have a merry day. I admit I had to look "merry" up in the dictionary, as I never hear anyone using "merry" (except, of course, Christmas-goers). Of all the definitions of "merry" that I could find—full of high-spirited gaiety, jolly, festive, brisk—I've decided that I prefer brisk, as in, have a brisk day, a day that goes by fast, one that is over quickly, one that soon delivers us from the tastelessness that is Christmas.

But I shouldn't be so cruel. My daughter loves Christmas. This one's for her.

Dead Animals (with Shining Eyes)

The painter Jeanne Socquet was fascinated by madness and the mentally ill. She was mesmerized by the way that "in lunatics the mouth is missing from the face." During the middle 20th century, Socquet went often to observe the patients at Clemenceau, a sanatorium not far from Paris. She also sketched the patients there, and in her sketches you can see that Socquet spent an obsessive amount of attention on their mouths. She said of their mouths that they "hang like dead animals on their faces."

All poets are lunatics. All poets are touched by the moon. (If you've ever been to a poetry reading, especially one in a small town or city, you know that this is true.) The irony of the impact the moon has on poetry and madness is interesting. For one group of lunatics the mouth is absent, dead. And for the other it won't stop singing. In fact, it often says too much (after all, what is a poem if not excessive use of language?).

Poetry has identified with the moon from its very beginning. The moon's journey across the night sky is symbolic of both loneliness and the span of a life. There's something about the moon that is fiercely true, and fiercely persistent in its truth. It surprises us, as if on seeing it we suddenly catch a glimpse of our own reflection. There we are, surrounded by darkness. Alone. Sad but shining, though not for long. Poetry's identification with the moon seems almost tautological. In fact, one wonders if poetry might even precede the moon.

Current scientific data dates the moon as being around 4.53 billion years old. By contrast, hominids are only 6 million years old. The first known poet is Enheduanna, a Mesopotamian priestess and princess who lived and wrote sometime around 2250 BCE. Poetry before that time is anonymous, written or sung by, presumably, humans. We're not sure when it started. For millennia, it was ephemeral, something like the wind. I've often wondered about a poetry that might have existed *before* humans.

Here's Mary Ruefle wondering something similar: "The great lu-nacy of most lyric poems is that they attempt to use words to convey what cannot be put into words. On the other hand, stars were the first text, the first instance of gabbiness; connecting the stars, making a pattern out of them, was the first story, sacred to storytellers."

Ancient cultures, including the Greeks and Romans, "discovered" or "divined" their myths by connecting the stars to form the shapes of gods. Those shapes formed along with the stories of those shapes. I imagine some stories already existed, and were only proven by the stars, while others came about as a result of the stars. I imagine also that no one cared much which came first, the stars or the stories in the stars. These ancient poets and storytellers literally read the stars. They found the stories written in the sky. They were readers more than they were writers. Call them diviners. In fact, humans didn't write any-thing down at all until around 3100 BCE. Humans didn't even speak language, and were therefore unable to *tell* stories, until 50,000 years ago.

Some linguists date the ability to speak language as early as 350,000 years ago, compatible with the migrations of Homo sapi-ens. Whenever it was, someone, at some point, looked up at a clear night sky, saw the moon, and saw the stars, and saw that there was po-etry playing about. And spoke or sang those poems, and those stories. Those poems and those stories that they found in the sky.

The constellation Lyra, for instance, is said by the Greeks to be the lyre of the mythical poet Orpheus. The Bacchantes accused Orpheus of dishonoring Dionysus, the god of wine, madness, theatre, and rit-ual madness. As punishment for this affront, the Bacchantes dismem-bered him, then threw his lyre (and his head) into the river Hebrus. Zeus rescued Orpheus' lyre and placed it in the night sky. So then, Or-pheus is the first poet? And Orpheus, after all, was human. He was a mythical human, perhaps, but still human.

But Orpheus learned the art of poetry from his mother, Calliope. Calliope was/is the goddess of eloquence and epic poetry. Is she the first poet? And if so, then how old are the gods and goddesses? I suppose that depends on whether you think the gods created us, or we created the gods . . .

Did someone teach Calliope how to sing, and what to sing? Was it Zeus, father of gods and humans? And, since Zeus placed the mythical Orpheus' lyre in the sky, and that lyre was the constellation Lyra, and the stars certainly predate humans, poetry then was already here when the first humans looked up.

". . . the moon was the first poem, in the lyric sense, an entity complete in itself, recognizable at a glance, one that played upon the emotions so strongly that the context of time and place hardly seemed to matter." (Ruefle)

Poets and lunatics feel the play of the moon in their hearts and minds . . . as does anyone and anything else on this earth.

The word "lunatic" has a rich place in the English language. It was first used to describe the mentally ill in the 1700s. It's derived from Latin, *luna*, moon. The Indo-European root—*leuk*—has many derivations, mostly meaning something like "to shine." Light, luminary, luminous, lunar, lunatic, luster, illustrate, lea, lucid, elucidate, translucent, and lynx are all derivatives of the same root, "*leuk*."

Lucifer also shares this root. Lucifer is the most radiant of angels, the bearer of light. In the same way a monster de*monstr*ates, lucifer e*luci*dates.

Limn is to describe, to depict by painting or drawing. A phillumenist is one who collects matchbooks or matches.

To be lunate is to be shaped like a crescent.

Sublunary is to be situated beneath the moon, as most of us are, unless you're "over the moon" for someone or something.

Lucubrate is to work not by moonlight, but by lamplight, a simulacrum of the moon.

Leuko means clear, white (like the moon). To have leukemia is to have an excess of white blood cells.

Lea means meadow, or "a place where (moon)light shines."

A lucid dream is one that is clear as moonlight.

Noctiluca are the bioluminescent dinoflagellates that cause the sea to shine at night in wild phosphorescence.

Lychnis means lamp and is a flower family that includes the campions.

A lynx is called a lynx because of its shining eyes.

The word lunatic is of course no longer considered appropriate to use in reference to the mentally ill, but I like the notion that a lunatic has wild, bright eyes and is touched by the moon. One no longer needs to go to a sanatorium to see them. At least not in the U.S. They are everywhere in every city. The neighborhood where I live is busy with them. The lynxes are everywhere, shouting out wild phosphorescence. The mentally ill wander the streets with impunity and disregard. They illuminate certain social issues we find difficult to solve, and often collect matches and lighters.

They are brilliant, and touched by the moon. Unfortunately, fentanyl, meth, hunger, and addiction darken them, dim them, and cause them to hang from the waist like dead animals in the parks, in doorways, between buildings, or in windrows waiting for meals outside churches.

It's safe to say that most of us in the liberal town I live in will find it offensive that Socquet went to observe the mentally ill, and sketch them. We here are quick to judge. And quick to be certain. But at least Socquet paid them some attention. After all, how do *we* treat our mentally ill? We don't. We ignore them if we can. We ignore them as if that were the humane thing to do.

Trigger Warning: High School

I don't remember high school. Thank God. That is, I try not to think of it. I mean, the actual high school part of it: classes, teachers' names, most of my classmates, etc. I'm not ashamed to say the thing I loved most about high school was looking out the window. Thirty years after the fact—the fact being high school—my secondary education has dissolved into insignificance. What seemed very important then, is now just a series of striations on a rocky cliff from which, if I look close enough at the sediment and fossilized bone, I can divine traumatic moments, triumphant mistakes, catastrophic events, loves won and lost, etc., but the impact of these events has dissipated over time, and their effects are no longer felt.

I suppose all of life is like this: seemingly much more important than it actually is. Specificity fans out into more general effects, concatenations become increasingly vague and untraceable.

When Alli entered high school, I felt like I entered it too. Again. At least, I found myself remembering things that I hadn't thought of in decades. It was impossibly stressful for her, as it was for me. She was a mess, as was I. The social maneuvering was horrific. She could hardly stand it. I could hardly stand hearing her tell me about it. It's an argument against evolution. A high school cafeteria is proof we haven't evolved as a species at all. We certainly haven't become more civilized.

I'm not sure why we continue to put our kids through this. The ills they learn seem to outweigh the values, which are lost in the cracks of hysterical hallways and overcrowded classrooms. It's a prison culture where the inhabitants are caged, anxious to escape, sexually frustrated, violent. Why subject our kids to such a volatile environment with such dubitable results?

And yet, over the next thirty years, it will for her, as it has for me, dissipate into insignificance. She'll hardly remember a thing. And then, perhaps, someday decades from now, as she drives away after dropping *her* child off a block and a half ("a little further please") from the high school, she'll shake her head and think, "how the hell did I survive that?"

Would You Like to Make a Donation?

The people that beg for money outside the grocery store have a new grift. Everyone calls them homeless, but most of them aren't. In fact, most of them live in the low-income housing unit around the corner. Our place isn't far from the grocery store, and it isn't far from the low-income building. We are all neighbors, and I know a few of them. I've been giving one or two of them money for years. This guy Greg gets a rent check every month from the government, and a little bit on top of it. But it's not enough to live on. Especially if you have an addiction. I don't mind buying Greg a beer, or chips or a soda, which is all he usually wants. He seems nice. Not too addicted. Just mildly so and a little off. I might describe myself the same way. I'm pretty sure my wife would.

Nearly all the people that hang out outside the grocery have an addiction. Most of them are high or drunk. Sometimes you see them nodding off on a fentanyl high. Often they're not even begging. They're partying. Partying might not be the right word. They're getting shit-faced together. Sometimes they have a radio, music, and they're all laughing and singing under the bus stop shelter. Sometimes partying *is* the right word.

Lately I've seen a couple of them, more than a few, selling flowers on the street. Greg doesn't do it, but some of the others do. Yesterday I saw one of them pulling crocosmia out of one of the gardens that I take care of. I'm an apartment manager and am responsible for nine buildings on the block. I manage nearly half the block. The buildings and the gardens, too.

I admit that when I saw this person yanking flowers out of the garden, I lost it. It wasn't the first time. I've seen it more and more. So, I regret to say, I snapped. I know it sounds ridiculous, but I yelled . . . well, I guess I didn't really yell . . . I opened the window and said, "excuse me!"

The culprit looked around but didn't see me.

"Excuse me!" I said again. "Please don't take those flowers."

"No one's using them," this person said, a woman with a limp and shoes that didn't match.

"Using them for what?" I said, confused.

She didn't answer. She picked a few more, and then left, grabbing some lavender sprigs on her way down the street. I was annoyed, but I also felt dumb for yelling at her.

Then last night around 6 o'clock I saw the same woman near the grocery store. She was sitting in a wheelchair and in front of her, on the sidewalk, were several jars and bottles. Each bottle had a small bouquet of flowers in it. I recognized the crocosmia and the lavender sprigs.

She was selling them.

"How much are you selling these for?" I asked.

"How much do you have?" she asked back.

"I think I recognize a few of them," I said.

"Lavender, rosemary, roses, some quince I think . . ." the woman was gesturing to each as any salesperson would do.

"Crocosmia."

"What?"

"Those are crocosmia, not quince."

"Okay, what you said, and a hydrangea, some daisies . . . we're taking donations, too."

"What do you mean, too?"

"I don't know. I guess just that we're taking donations. You can donate," the woman said.

"Donate to what?"

"To buy the flowers."

"Donate to buy the flowers?"

"Yes, to the beauty of the neighborhood."

"To the beauty of the neighborhood," I said. "Where do you get your flowers?"

"We collect them."

"Who's we?"

"I am."

"You are we?"

"Yes. I collect them and we sell them to people to take home to their spouse, or to put on the dining room table."

"That's very kind of you," I said.

"Would you like to make a donation?"

"To your noble cause?"

"Yes, if you like. To our noble cause, for the sake of the flowers in the neighborhood."

"You're good," I said, and I actually considered donating. "If I donate, can I have my flowers back?"

"What flowers?"

"The ones you took from my garden."

"We didn't take these."

"I saw you."

"We collect them in the neighborhood. All of these were donated to us," she said, and moved her arm in a sweeping motion to indicate all the flowers in front of her.

"Ah . . . I see."

"So do you want to make a donation?"

"I think I already have."

Just then a young woman with a child walked up and looked at all the different bouquets. The child was very attracted to them, and kept trying to pull the flowers out of their soup cans and bottles.

"Hello," the woman said.

"Hello," said the flower seller.

"Which one should we get, Lu Lu?" The woman said to the child.

"I like this one," Lu Lu said, and knocked three bouquets over as she grabbed a fourth.

"Oh be careful, honey. Don't knock over the nice lady's flowers . . . I'm so sorry."

"It's fine," said the flower seller, "what a cute little girl you are!"

The little girl smiled.

"How much for this one?" the woman gestured at the bouquet in Lu Lu's hands.

"Fifteen dollars."

"Fifteen dollars!" I said.

Lu Lu's mother looked at me. Then turned to the flower seller, "I only have a twenty, but please, keep the change."

"Bless you," the flower seller said, "and bless your little Lu Lu."

"Jeezus Christ," I said.

Lu Lu's mother gave me a nervous look and pulled her daughter towards her, then they said thank you and walked off. Lu Lu kept turning around and waving at the flower seller, who smiled and waved back.

When the mother and child disappeared into the grocery store, the woman stood up and grabbed a large duffle bag from behind the wheelchair. She pulled all the flowers out of their bottles and cans, and threw everything into the duffle bag.

"What are you doing?" I said.

"I have to meet someone."

"Who?"

"None of your business. Who are you anyway?"

"You stole my flowers," I said lamely.

"We don't steal flowers," she said.

"Why do you keep saying 'we'?"

"Look, I have to go. Do you want to make a donation or not?"

"To what?"

"To me."

"Why?"

"I don't know. For the same reason that woman and her little kid made a donation."

"This is crazy," I said.

"We put the flowers out, and people buy them . . . or they make a donation. What's so crazy about that?"

"I don't know. Don't you see?"

"I think you're crazy," the flower seller said. "I think you need to get a life."

"Me?"

"Yes, you. I'm done with this," she put the duffle bag on the wheelchair, and I watched her as she pushed it away.

Greg came up then, eating a bag of Funyuns, "Buy me a can of beer?"

"Sure."

Hi Mom

We are the ones who are buried alive. By we, I mean all of us. By buried, I mean dropped here, into this world, this house of mirrors where you cannot see the same you twice. But no one will blame you if you act as if you do. If you act as if you do see the same you twice. If you act as if there is a you, as if you have a self. "For everything tends towards itself." We all do it, and—let's be honest—it's easier to pretend nothing has changed, we haven't aged. It's easier to pretend you are the same you twice, that you have a static self, a true you. Your true self.

I'm trying to be as simple as I can. Let me start over:

My mother came to visit. I hadn't seen her in a few years. Five, I guess. Maybe more. When I picked her up at the airport, I noticed immediately how old she looked. Like an old woman. But I didn't say anything, out of consideration for her. I just smiled. I hugged her. After our hug, she looked at me, then grabbed my face and said, "oh honey, look at how old you are now."

I laughed. She laughed. We laughed and laughed and laughed.

VII.

THAT SHALLOW BROOK

*In which the author experiences death
for the first time, then
several more times*

One Last Joke

My grandfather was dying. He was on the hospital bed, very pale. Still breathing but pale as death, or so we thought, we would soon learn death's actual color.

We came to say goodbye. My grandmother called us all in, and our whole family drove to the hospital. She said it was "time to pull the plug." I was sixteen years old. I didn't really understand how anyone could pull someone else's plug. I was told he agreed, but I couldn't believe it. I didn't believe it. Who on earth would agree to that!

He was still talking, but just barely. He even seemed to be in good spirits, which was typical of my grandfather. He was always in good spirits. He would've smiled before a firing squad. I suppose that's exactly where he was now.

"Tell me a joke," he said to my little brother. Everyone loved my little brother. There were four of us kids, but everyone loved him the best. All of us.

"Tell me a joke," my grandfather said again, and laughed weakly when he said it, as if the mere thought of a joke already contained a bit of the punchline.

My little brother *was* funny. His jokes weren't very good. In fact, they were mostly terrible. But he was funny. Somehow his jokes were funny even though they weren't very good. He was a ham. We all thought he took after my grandfather.

I was a little shocked he wanted to hear a joke at such a moment. One last joke? It better be a good one. I knew it wouldn't be. It might be funny, but it wouldn't be a good joke, not a joke good enough to be the last joke he'd ever hear.

I was glad he hadn't asked me. My jokes, I thought, were better than my brother's, but it didn't matter. My brother was still much funnier. My grandfather just wanted to laugh. He wanted to laugh one more time before he died. He didn't care about the writing. He just wanted to laugh.

My oldest sister started crying. I was very confused. I didn't know what to do. Should I cry, too? Was he really dying? What did that even mean?

Three days before my grandfather asked my brother to tell him a joke, we were bowling. He took us bowling. He taught us how to get enough spin on the ball to bend it right into the pocket, the pocket between the first and second pins. If you could slide the ball into that pocket, you would get a strike nearly every time. The pins would explode.

He showed us what to do. "Five steps," he said. "Keep your eyes on that second arrow painted on the lane. Don't even look at the pins. Just look at the arrows, look at that second arrow. Look how close it is. That's easy to hit. You can definitely hit that arrow. It's so close."

"Now," he said, "when you release the ball, just act like you're shaking someone's hand. When you follow through," he showed us without a ball in his hand, his arm swung up and his palm was facing to the left, "like this, just like you're shaking someone's hand. A handshake . . ." I shook his hand. He laughed. "Now watch."

He grabbed a ball, took five steps, and threw the ball with the handshaking follow-through. "See it hit the second arrow. See how it's swerving . . ." The ball crashed into the pocket between the first and second pins and they exploded. They didn't all fall down, but they did explode. "Hmm . . ." he said, "oh well. You don't always get a strike."

He took us out for burgers afterwards. He ordered two double cheeseburgers, a side of fries, and a large coke. Three days later he had a catastrophic heart attack. He somehow survived. He survived but his right ventricle blew apart. He'd bowled a strike. Or close to one. Maybe it was a 7–10 split. The doctors said the fact that he was still breathing was a miracle, but there was no way he'd be able to survive the surgery. They could probably keep him alive for a day or two, but the pain would be immense. They advised pulling the plug.

"Tell me a joke," he said again from the hospital bed.

My little brother had a frightened look on his face. Both my sisters were crying. My oldest sister was nearly hysterical. I was still confused and just taking it all in. I didn't know what to do. It was like having a weird dream. A terrible dream. Our parents, and grandmother, were out in the hall talking to the doctors.

"Poppo what happened?" my oldest sister said, through tears.

"It will all be fine," he said. "Don't worry about me. It will all be fine." His voice was quiet, and he was struggling to get the words out.

My sister sobbed.

"Please," he said to my brother, "tell me a joke."

My brother now looked terrified. Tears welled in both of his eyes. He looked back and forth from my sister to my grandfather, who moved his arm. His hand fell against mine and I grabbed it. It was cold. Stiff and cold.

"Poppo," I said.

He looked at me and smiled.

"Poppo," I said again, "why did the chicken cross the road?"

"Why did what?"

"Why did the chicken cross the road?"

"What chicken?"

My sisters laughed through their sobs. My brother laughed, too, his eyes glazed with suspended tears.

"Just a chicken. It's a joke. I'm telling you a joke."

"Yes, tell me a joke," he said.

"I am," I said.

"Okay," he said and closed his eyes.

"Why did the chicken cross the road?"

"Why did the chicken what?" he asked, opening his eyes, and my siblings laughed again. We all laughed, and my grandfather smiled and then closed his eyes again.

"Why did the chicken cross the road?" I said again.

His hand went limp in mine. It was cold. His hand was somehow both limp and stiff, like clay, and very cold. You could tell he wasn't there anymore. He was somewhere else. He was on the other side.

"Poppo?" I said, lamely, "why did the chicken cross the road?"

"Why," my sister cried, but it wasn't really a question.

Parable of the Stone Mason

I worked for a while on a crew that built patios. Stone patios. It was hard work, but I liked it. Our foreman was extremely skilled, and I respected his work. He was more than just a patio maker. A stone mason, I guess you'd call him. Of course, most of what we did was make patios out of stone, but we built some stone walls, too. He seemed like he could do anything with a hammer and chisel.

We had saws, too, with diamond blades to cut the stone, as well as the hammers and chisels, all shapes and sizes of chisels. When I first started working for him, he showed me one of the chisels and said it was his favorite, and that he mostly used it, exclusively.

"Mostly or exclusively?" I said.

"I don't know," he said. "I use it a lot." He looked at it very fondly. You could see he loved it. He said that every stone asks questions, sometimes more than one, and this particular chisel always knew the answer. I liked the way he said that. I liked the way he looked at it while he was talking about it, how he held the chisel in his hand. "Here," he said, "you can almost feel it buzzing, almost like it's alive." He handed it to me, and I held it. It was warm from him holding it, and though it was small it was heavy. I tried to feel it humming. It was an odd moment, one I didn't really understand, but I admired the way he talked about his trade, and his tools.

A year later he killed himself. It was a big shock. He seemed so content. No one on the crew saw it coming. His wife had left him, and she'd taken their three-year-old daughter with her. He never mentioned it the whole time we worked together. No one knew. I guess things just sort of fell apart from there, and eventually he couldn't take it anymore. I didn't notice a thing. He didn't talk much, but that wasn't unusual, none of us talked much while we were working. He just cut and hammered and chiseled the stone, and placed it perfectly every time.

Maybe content isn't the right word to describe him, but he was certainly "in tune." He was simple, I guess. Not dumb, not dumb at all. He liked plants and stones and sports. He was, I guess you'd say, connected to the simple things in life: surfaces, shapes, textures. And he knew everything about stones: where a fissure ran through the rock, where the coal veins would cause a stone to fracture at some point in the future. And where also, he once told me, a piece of sandstone lacked silica—a kind of natural cement—and therefore was too mealy to hold together. He could look at a stone and know immediately that it wouldn't hold, that it would crumble over time. Or see by the grain if it would break, given enough pressure. He could tell that certain stones, with little warning, would just snap.

I guess he taught me to see it, too. But sometimes you just can't tell.

I'm not sure what to say about him. What use is a life like that? His daughter too young to remember him. An ex-wife who despises him. What am I supposed to do with the memory of him? Hold it? Forget it? Hand it to someone else to hold, if only for a minute?

We worked a little longer on that crew, then it just ended. When I left I took the chisel. I still have it. I used it for a while but now it's in the closet. I know exactly where it is.

Of Cynicism and Unsavory Wisdom

Sure, I've tried it. A few times. A couple times I got pretty close. Back when I was a teenager. That seems like a good time to do it.

"It's not a bad longing, the longing to die. It's not a disastrous longing," says Marguerite Duras, the princess of darkness (or, as she might prefer, the proletarian of darkness . . . and of cynicism and unsavory wisdom).

But I didn't succeed. I'm glad I failed. Those were difficult psychological times. (Duras again: "The void you discover in your teens— nothing can ever undo that discovery.") It's much better now to contend with a sort of vague (almost pastoral) longing to die. There's something close, cozy in it, like staring out the window on a rainy day.

I suppose that's what life is like sometimes, you can't really experience it. You can only watch it, remember it. This is a bizarre flaw of the human psyche. A cruel contradiction. When you're engaged and living entirely, you're mostly unconscious. Being thoughtless is, perhaps, the best way to be. Except you don't realize you're having such a great time because you're not thinking, you're thoughtless. Thus, phrases like "lost in my work," "forgetting myself," etc.

"How was the beach?"

"It was a dream."

It was a dream because your consciousness couldn't process it. Why not? What's so difficult about a beach? It's not Nietzsche or calculus. It's sitting on your ass at the beach.

But somehow it passes. It slips like water through your hands. And very soon all you can do is remember being there. Sometimes the memory's even better than the actual day at the beach. In fact, it usually is.

The trick, it would seem to me, is to attempt to remember the thing you are doing in the present. I've tried, and it's nearly possible. Nearly. The problem is, in order to do so you have to stop, you have to think of yourself acting and therefore cease to be engaged in the act. You are no longer sitting at the beach. You are recognizing yourself sitting at the beach. Essentially you are staring out the window on a rainy day. This sometimes makes me want to die. Death seems like it would be a very immediate way of living. All encompassing. Whole. You would not be stuck between two different realities, unable to fully experience either. Or rather, you wouldn't be on the outside, looking at death, you'd just be dead. No more looking. No more longing. At last a pure and absolute engagement.

I admire the dead. I think about my grandparents a lot. I knew a couple of my great grandparents when I was young. I guess I don't really think of them as being dead. Or maybe it's that the word "dead" means something different to me, something less final, something still in this world. They're not in some other world, they're in some other part of this world. I admire them. I even envy them, as you might envy a successful person. Or someone very happy. Someone enlightened. All their longing gone. All their million microbes harmonious at last. Undisturbed. Dead.

SAINT JOAN

As of July, I have been in this town nearly thirty years. When I say "nearly," I mean exactly. How depressing.

I also mean, by "nearly," not really thirty years at all. Far from it. I have been places since I moved here, even lived in other places. In Australia twice, and Mexico, Taiwan, and Colorado for a year, the Bay Area for six months. Not to mention various smaller trips—two months in Italy, three months working on a fishing boat in the Aleutian Islands. Michigan, Louisville, New Orleans. New York, San Francisco, Chicago, Indiana, etc. Also, all the myriad flights from the city to all the myriad small, depressed towns in the mountains or on the coast, to break up the monotony of living in the same town, the same neighborhood. These little trips, unfortunately, never work. They are like gum that loses its flavor almost immediately after arriving.

Anyway, as of July I have been in this town thirty years. More or less. How depressing. That's long enough to be a rock-star overdose, a suicide of Saturn's return. Thirty years . . . it's a whole person's life. And yet I had another life before it. At least two in fact. I suppose that makes me old. I suppose I *am* old. Pushing fifty (soon I'll be *pulling* fifty!).

From this apartment alone I've stared out the window every morning for twenty years. Every morning describing the gardens across the street, the dogwood and coral bark maple, the darker shade the bricks turn when it rains on the brownstones. Every morning the same joggers jogging dumbly by. Think of it! The jogger bouncing by twenty years ago is now a middle-aged woman, an old man, probably not jogging anymore. Their backs are probably sore. Their knees and heels. Maybe they're dead. Like Joan.

Joan died a few years ago. Joan who was seventy, once, or close to it, when I moved in. Joan who used to wear a huge red raincoat and walk down to the bar on the corner to have a martini every night. Saint Joan, we called her. Not because she was a saint, but because she drank a martini every night until the day she died. It took her over a half-hour to walk a single block. She'd stop at every light pole and rest, leaning against it. To rest and admire the roses, lavender, lithodora. In pain, winded, all for her martini. Now that's devotion! That's sacrifice!

When we got back from the Midwest one summer, she was gone. Some guys were doing drywall in her apartment. I asked them if they knew anything about the woman who used to live there, but they didn't. "We're just the drywall guys," they said.

I still see her ghost, though less and less, haunting the sidewalks on her way (the ghost's) to the bar on the corner to drink her haunted martini. Her huge red raincoat still floats like a kinetic azalea down the street.

I used to think she liked to talk to me, but then I realized she just couldn't walk very far without stopping to rest. Sometimes when she stopped to rest, I'd be standing there, and she'd talk to me. I guess I took it personally. Meaning, I thought she liked to talk to me. I liked to talk to her.

Oh fuck the passage of time! I don't buy it or believe in it. What if it's a myth? What if we just recycle? What if we're perennials, like lilies or liriope? Same flowers every spring. New joggers to replace the old. New Joans. I know she's dead but who's to say she isn't just at a different bar, drinking her martini, on some other corner, in some other place.

You Can Say Goodbye Now

Sometimes I remember it like this: one day my grandfather stuffed two double cheeseburgers down his throat and died. I know because I was there. I had seven single hamburgers with ketchup and mustard. I was young so I didn't die. I was a teenager. It sounds crazy, but I could eat that much. Then. But my grandfather . . . well, you can't just keep adding cheeseburgers to yourself for seventy years and not expect to one day die.

He didn't die immediately. We went bowling first. He was a great bowler. He bowled with grace, which to me was always more important than the score. I loved watching him bowl. So tall and so living, breathing. Like a dancer or the bass player in a jazz band. He seemed to remove himself and let the bowling ball flow through him. I'll never forget it. I hope I never forget it.

When he took us home, he was still alive. And when I waved goodbye, he was alive. And he drove off alive and I thought nothing of it. I never saw him again. I never saw him alive again.

That night, while we were watching "The Cosby Show," he died. He wasn't watching "The Cosby Show" I don't think, though I guess I don't know what he was watching. Back then, in the '80s, everyone watched something. You sort of had to.

Anyway, we were watching "The Cosby Show" at our house, and my grandparents were watching something else (I guess) at their condo on the East Side. My grandma said he poured two martinis down his throat and died. No one argued with her. We all accepted it. They were of the ratpack generation. Cocktails were part of every evening. I suppose I'm third generation ratpack.

My grandmother called from the hospital. My grandfather was already dead. My father was on the phone with her for what seemed like forever. He even turned off the TV. That's how we knew something terrible had happened. After some time, we all piled in the station wagon and went to the hospital. I had never been to a hospital before, except to get my broken arm fixed, but I don't remember it. I think I was in shock.

When we got to the hospital, he was still dead. I thought he wouldn't be, but he was. He still was and he still is. He's been a very stubborn man in that way. My mother said, "would you like to hold his hand?"

I was surprised and didn't know what to do. I was in shock again, I think. I just let her lead me over to him and she grabbed my hand and grabbed my grandfather's hand and put his hand in mine. It was heavy and cold and I held it but was very confused about why I was holding it and what I was supposed to feel. I was scared. And profoundly sad, but the sadness was still in the shock place.

"Would you like to say goodbye?" my mom asked me.

"Okay," I said, but I just stood there, holding the hand and looking at the head that looked like my grandfather's head but clearly wasn't. Clearly was something else now. Something terrible and nothing like the head that I'd seen on top of the elegant body rolling the bowling ball down the lane and sliding ever so slightly across the polished wood floor.

"Go ahead," my mother said, "you can say goodbye now."

Death and Failure and Bristlecone Pines

I admit I think of death as a kind of failure. A tragedy, to be sure, but also a failure. I'm just being honest. I've tried to be more accepting. But I can't.

The geranium in the balcony box, for instance. It came back again this spring, and is blooming now in May. The verbena, though, didn't make it. It failed to. I planted them both at the same time, in the same way, under the same circumstances. One makes it through the winter, one fails to do so.

I saw a rat that had been run over by a car. It had been there for some time. It was flat against the pavement. All of its guts squeezed out through the hole in its side where it burst like a balloon. Many cars had run over it. I was riding my bike, and I saw it, and I took a picture of it with my phone. I know it sounds crazy, but it wasn't for any sadistic reason, it was more like a memento mori: just one thing I'd noticed dead in a sea of death all around.

I'm not trying to be insensitive. None of us have much control, ultimately. But it does seem to be a failure of certain species that they can't achieve greater longevity. Mayflies have only hours on this earth, a day at most. While a Great Basin Bristlecone Pine can live for thousands of years. The Bristlecones, to me, are a great success.

When I say certain species, I suppose I also mean individuals of certain species (see rat above). A mayfly who lives an hour longer is as much of a success as the pine that makes it a few decades more.

And what is *our* problem! Most of us, we humans, if we're lucky, make it seventy or eighty years. That's it! Randomly flipping through the dictionary, I see that Pat Nixon lived to be eighty-one. Richard Nixon also eighty-one. George Mason (American Revolutionary) died at sixty-seven. Eleanor Roosevelt was ninety. Even Socrates lived to be seventy-one. In the US, life expectancy for women is eighty-two, for men it's seventy-seven. It seems to me we've failed if we haven't been able to elongate our lives more than a few years since Socrates, who lived over 2300 years ago. Sure, Socrates was exceptional in many ways, including longevity, and humans overall are living longer now than ever before. But obviously there's a limit to what our bodies can handle—the bodies of men, women, and bristlecone pines. What our bodies can handle before they fail.

But we've more than doubled our life expectancy in the last 100 years, you'll say. Science and medicine now allow a human on this planet to live an average of 73 years, whereas in 1900 it was only 31. Thirty-one! Even Jason would've been an old man. Surely that is a great success. A triumph of humankind's will to survive. And, of course, that is true and you are right.

But still, I think of death as a failure.

Ultimately, we can't escape us. We're stuck, fixed in the wax of our biological limitations. Fossilized in the mud of our genetic riverbeds. Evolution can only take us so far. And all we can do (if we're lucky) is fill out the full potential of our measly seventy or eighty years. Bask in the sun that long, before the porchlight goes out, again, forever.

What Use Is a Body Like This?

We were on the island. My grandmother and I. Her husband (my grandfather) of forty-something years had died some years earlier, and she wanted to come out for a visit.

I rented a car and picked her up from the airport. We left the city the next day. A long loop around the state. Two states. Part of this loop we spent up in the islands.

It was going well enough, considering we hadn't seen each other in over five years, during which time I'd become something like an adult. I was twenty-six. I wasn't living on the street anymore. I was in college. I hadn't been in jail for a while. I worked in a library. It was summer.

She bought all the meals, paid for the hotels, the car, the gas, etc. My job was to drive, to book our lodgings, find places to eat, hair-dressers, etc. and every evening to make sure she got her dry martini on the rocks with a twist.

It was going well enough.

The lodgings on the island were a bit more rustic than she was used to. There was no air-conditioning.

"You won't need it," I said, "it's not like the Midwest out here."

"But my asthma . . ." she said. "I'm worried I'll have an attack."

"It won't be hot. Especially not at night."

"I think we need to find another hotel."

I left her in her room and went down to the lobby. The host there told me they didn't have any air-conditioned rooms. "It doesn't get hot here," she said.

"I know, but my grandmother, she's worried about her asthma."

"Let's see," she said, and typed something into her computer. I thought maybe she was trying to find a room with A/C. "It says here the low temperature tonight will be 53. Does she know that?"

"I don't know but she's freaking out."

"Tell her she can leave the windows open."

"Yes, I know, I did. She's worried about bugs."

"We don't really have bugs here."

"I told her that, too. She's from the Midwest. She doesn't understand."

"I see," the woman said. She wasn't really interested in the conversation. "I can give you a fan."

"That would be great. Thanks."

When I got back up to the room, the door was open. My grandmother was lying on the bed with the curtains drawn. It was two in the afternoon.

"Room service." I said quietly. "I brought you a fan."

She said nothing.

"Are you okay?"

"I think I just need to rest a while. Please turn the fan on. I'll be fine after I rest for an hour or so. Then we can figure out what to do."

"Can I get you anything else?"

"No no. I just need to rest. You know your grandfather was a wonderful man . . ."

"I know," I said.

"He always took care of me."

I left her there in the room and drove the rental car along the narrow lanes of the island. I wound along the coast, then cut across the farmlands and cattle fields on the interior, went through a patch of forest that stretched all the way to the other side of the island. The island wasn't that big. It was beautiful, but I didn't think I could live on it. At least not very long.

I stopped in a park overlooking the Strait. You could see other islands. Maybe Canada, too? I wasn't sure. Could you tell just by looking if it was Canada or not? Or would it look the same? Would the land be nicer? The cliffs less severe, the hillsides more gentle? I couldn't tell.

I sat on a bench and stared out at the sea, not really thinking much. It's nice not to think, I thought.

A few sea gulls were screaming at something. At each other or at something I couldn't see. What were they so upset about? Living here? On this coast? Food everywhere on the rocks below. Little fish by the millions to eat. What was wrong with them? They definitely didn't seem content. In fact, the opposite. Squawking and shrieking as they circled over me.

Maybe I was sitting by their nest. I picked up a rock and threw it at one of them. I missed. Not even close really. I don't think the bird even knew I'd thrown it. It was glancing at me, and it still screamed, but it didn't look like it knew what I was or what I was doing. It didn't seem to be able to read my motions. To it, whether I was sitting or throwing a rock was basically the same thing. For an instant I had the impression that I was the seagull seeing me, seeing the wingless thing in clothes. What use was a body like that? Unflying. Unfeathered, cold and wet.

Then it was over. I was me again, and I really was cold and wet. The gulls were anxious, they wouldn't shut up. It wasn't relaxing being there, listening to them. In fact, it was kind of stressful. But of course they're screaming, I thought, why wouldn't they be? Aren't there a hundred thousand things to scream about in this world?

Later, at a restaurant, when she ordered her dry martini on the rocks with a twist, I asked for one, too. I told her about the island, how beautiful it was. I told her about the park I found and how you couldn't tell if the islands across the Strait were part of Canada or just more islands.

"Did you see any Canadians on them?" she asked, and we laughed.

"How would I recognize them?"

"I don't know," she said, "I always thought Canadians would just be happier. Sometimes I act like your grandfather didn't die. I imagine he's just traveling. Maybe he's in Canada."

"Hmm," I said, and we were quiet for a while. "I did see a bunch of angry seagulls screaming and whining and making a mess of the serenity of the place. I'm not sure what their problem was," I said.

"American seagulls. . ." she said.

"Ha. Yeah I guess so."

"Life isn't always easy," she said, and I was surprised by the solemnity in her voice. "Your grandfather loved seagulls. He loved anything that had to do with the sea . . ."

I raised my glass to hers, and she smiled. "Here's to the sea and seagulls," I said. I never told her that I threw the rock. What would I have said? I wasn't even sure why I'd thrown it.

Quick, To Other Forms!

"Real wisdom's when your dead twin suddenly walks up to you."

—Shen-hui

Jason died when he was in his thirties. I didn't find out until recently. I made the mistake of searching for him online. I'm not sure why I thought of him, or why I decided to search for him, but when I did, I found his obituary.

When we were teenagers, Jason and I used to talk about death and what might happen to us after we died. I am a cynic in this regard. When it comes to the afterlife. I am a cynic now, but I used to be much worse. I suppose as I've gotten older, I've progressed from absolute nihilism to a kind of temperate cynicism. I agree with Bertrand Russell: "I believe that when I die I'll rot, and nothing of my ego remain." And Pascal: "The last act is bloody, however fine the rest of the play. They throw earth over your head and it is finished forever." This perspective seems pretty pragmatic to me. Even refreshing.

My feelings about death have softened over the years. I'm not exactly sure why. I suppose I've softened. Not that I'm one of these delusional reincarnationists. The best, most optimistic view I can accept now is that, maybe, we are subsumed into other physical bodies, both animate and not, that exist on this planet. "Of bodies changed to other forms I tell," begins Ovid in his *Metamorphoses*, written sometime around the year 15 BCE. Theories of the afterlife haven't improved much since then as far as I'm concerned (and in fact have mostly become more ridiculous). So I subscribe to Ovid: we die, and when we do we change, particle by particle, "to other forms." Even if those forms are just ash, dust, dirt. Something eats the dirt. Maybe a worm. Then a bird eats a worm . . . gradually we're dispersed, dissolved and dismembered into other forms. How nice. How simple, cyclical, and complete.

You could extend this to our consciousness as well: bits of it here, bits of it there. Consciousness, after all, is just made up of cells, little bits of physical matter that spark and synapse and fool us into thinking we are something more than, say, kinetic fire hydrants.

Jason always seemed more interested in the subject than I was. Maybe he knew he wouldn't live long. Maybe he intended to die. He was always reaching hard (irritably, Keats has said) after the truth. Or at least for an answer that he could live with, that he could die with. Perhaps he was looking for a way out. A way out of the unsolvable riddle: there is a game, no one asks you if you want to play, at some point you realize you're already playing it, you can't win the game, you can only lose, and there's no way to stop playing until you lose, when you lose you die. I would tell him to relax, the game will take care of itself. That would end the conversation for a while, but then he'd return to searching, doubting, theorizing. Neither of us had any religious dogma to fall back on. Not that we wanted any. We were hoping for something more believable.

"I've got it," he said to me one day.

"Got what?"

"I've figured it out."

"Okay . . ."

"It's really just a simple exercise in logic."

"How so?"

"All is darkness before you're born, right?"

"I don't know, I don't remember."

"Exactly. You don't remember because it was all darkness. There's nothing to remember."

"Okay . . ."

"And all is darkness after we die, right?"

"I'll hear you out . . ."

"So you go from darkness, to light, to darkness again . . ."

"Okay . . .'

"So it must be that, if you go from darkness to light, and then return to darkness, it's possible you also then return to light. It's just like the earth spinning, catching the sun and then losing it again: night, day, night again, day again . . . and so on, forever!"

He was very excited.

"I like it," I said, though I didn't. I much preferred Ovid's bodies changing into other forms.

Then he died.

It's been almost ten years now. Long enough, perhaps, for the darkness to turn back into light.

I think about that conversation sometimes. And even though I don't believe it, sometimes I'll see someone and think, maybe that's Jason. Not Jason but maybe inside of that person there's some of the darkness that used to be his light. Used to be his light, then was darkness, and now is light again.

But then, almost immediately, I think, nah, probably not. I prefer to see him in no particular person or thing, to just see him in everything.

Someday We Wouldn't Be Sick

We were sick. It was the whole house. Liz and I and my daughter. All of us.

First it was just Alli, and I was bringing her vitamin C, cough drops, juice. She stayed home from school. I canceled some appointments, stayed home from work, took care of her. She wanted to hear me play "all the songs you know on guitar." I got the book out with the songs I'd printed out over the years. There were a lot, a few hundred at least. Most of them I don't play anymore. Most of them are from when she was little, that period after my marriage fell apart, before Liz, when it was just Alli and I living here. I used to sit in the bathroom and play songs for her while she took a bath. All kinds of songs. Sometimes she'd sing with me, but mostly she'd just play with her plastic animals and whisper dialogue between the tiger and the monkey, the giraffe and the skunk.

Anyway, that first day I played for her, and sang for her, until she said she wanted to go to sleep.

The next day I woke up sick. It was a Saturday and Liz brought us vitamin C, cough drops, juice. Alli was in her room, and I was on the couch out front. She watched some shows on her school computer, and I read the Pete Hamill novel I'd been putting off because (despite myself) I tend to feel like novels are beside the point. "But so what? What's so great about the point?" I said to myself, trying to convince myself that reading fiction isn't a waste of time. I picked up the Hamill book and read it. I didn't like it. I tried, but I just couldn't get over the seemingly arbitrary fictional plot. I mean, any character could do anything at any point in the story. There were no consequences. No obligations to reality. To truth. You could just say anything, anything at all. Fiction is ridiculous.

Liz went to work.

This went on for a couple days. I finished the book. Terrible. Completely fabricated ending. Probably supposed to be "magical realism."

I felt bad, though, that I felt that way about Pete Hamill, so I started rereading a book of his non-fiction. Much better.

Then Liz got sick. I brought everyone vitamin C, cough drops, juice. Then I went back to the couch. Alli was watching shows in her room. I had Hamill's non-fiction. Liz was reading course material from her teaching program in the bedroom.

This went on for a couple days. I watched the people outside going to work. I could see Norma cleaning the building across the street. Gregory and Archer on their bikes. Babette getting home from school. The neighborhood was proceeding as usual. Going on without us. Everything looked normal.

I knew someday we wouldn't be sick. Someday we'd be dead. Someday we'd be gone and all these people doing all the things they do would just keep on doing them. Then they too would die, and other people would do the things that the dead ones had done: go to work, come home from school, clean buildings, ride bikes, get sick, die. I knew this because of Diane. She used to live next door. And Rosin, who lived downstairs. They both died. And then there's Andrew and Jerome and Jesse and a hundred other people, thousands, who at one point lived on our block. I'd see them for a while and then they'd move away. Some of them I'm sure are dead now. Others might be, I don't know. Either way, I don't think about them anymore. I don't even remember who they were.

The Dahlias and the Forest Fire Smoke

Lately, in September, the air here is brown. A kind of gray-brown (if that's a thing), that you don't ever see anywhere else. Or anytime else. The color of a finch that's been hit by a car. Or the color of a cremation victim. (Maybe "victim" isn't the right word for someone who chooses cremation over burial . . . maybe the right word is cremation *patron*?)

The forest fires have become an annual occurrence. A festival of death and depression that clogs the lungs and poisons the blood. Our phones now tell us the Air Quality Index, in case you want to "stay indoors." Particulate matter browns the air, shortens the life, settles on the windowsills and floors, car hoods, piano keys. If you leave a book on the coffee table, you will see it when you pick it up: there beneath it, in the shape of the book, a negative space of clean. If not of clean, then at least of dustlessness, ashlessness, filth and forest meal all around everywhere. People wear masks outside. It's depressing.

But you have to live your life. You can't hide. Even if there are, increasingly, more and more reasons to hide. This is the crux, right? As there become more and more reasons to hide, it also becomes more and more imperative to ignore those things and live your life. There's more urgency.

If it wasn't certain before, it is now: we will die. And soon! The memento mori are piling up, and have now ceased to be mere memento. Mori is everywhere, no need to be reminded of it.

Every September, like clockwork, the forests burn and the skies fill up, and our lungs fill up with them, our veins pulse with poison blood . . . but September is also when the dahlias bloom, and on Saturdays we walk up to the park to see them. We breathe it all in. We stare deep into the weird and wild, astral blossoms. What else are we to do? Hide? Where? And to what end? To reach another September? Lately, in September, the air here is brown.

A Wall Built on Philosophical Grounds

"From now on, it's all pure again . . . whatever *it* is."

— Issa

I got a job. It sort of fell into my lap, as jobs sometimes do. And I have a rule, I guess, a personal philosophy, to accept the things that fall into my lap. As if they are opportunities fated to me. Opportunities I shouldn't question. That I should just accept. Who am I to question fate or feel that I know a better way?

I should probably point out that I don't believe in fate. What can I say? A human body is rotten with contradictions. This I also accept. This has also, in a way, fallen into my lap.

Anyway, I was at the library. I was leaving the library—having just checked out a book by Polanyi that my brother says, for him at least, "explains everything." I was leaving the library when I was stopped by a man with a bike helmet on.

"Oh hi," he said, as he moved to let me through the door.

"Hi," I said, "thanks."

"Are you the one who built the gardens on 85th?"

I should mention that mental illness is a big problem in our neighborhood, and a lot of us have become used to nonsensical conversations, so I said "I might be that person . . . who are you?"

"I also live on 85th," he said.

"Aah," I said.

"Look, I'm in a bit of hurry now, but I'd love to hire you to build a garden in front of my place." He was wearing a high-stretch bicycle outfit. I harbor a general suspicion toward people who wear outfits of any kind, especially outfits that are genital-forward.

"Um hmm."

"Would you be interested in that?"

"Perhaps," I said, "we can discuss it sometime."

"I can pay you."

"That would be required," I said.

"Of course," he said.

"Of course," I said.

"Of course," he said, "great, when you have time, we should talk." He gave me his phone number then, and I walked away.

I only live a few blocks from the library, and when I got home, I saw the same man in the bike outfit ride past my building and pull into a driveway down the street. The area in front of his house was small. I could easily build a garden there, I thought. I would wait a few days, and then call him.

We met on a Saturday, and stood out front of his place discussing what could be done. I proposed a low stone wall with various plants trailing over it, behind the wall a few perennials and flowering shrubs, and a few larger things beyond that. A camellia, a pieris, maybe a dwarf magnolia. "There are many options," I said.

"Great," he said.

"The wall will look fantastic," I said, "but it will cost money."

"Of course," he said.

"And you'll want irrigation, too. It will take time."

"Of course," he said.

"It will take time to do it right," I said.

"Of course," he said.

"Of course," I said, "I'll write up a proposal and get it to you soon."

"No hurry," he said.

"Great," I said.

A few days later I sent him a proposal. It was June, mid-June, and I could start the job July 1. It would take six weeks or more. This meant that most, nearly all, of my summer would be spent building this wall, installing irrigation, and planting this garden. No vacation. No trips to the beach or the river or mountains. No nights of drinking wine and listening to records until 3 a.m. I'd be working all summer, and if not working I'd be exhausted from working. Every time someone called, I'd have to say, "I don't think I can make it, I'm working."

I added a little extra to the bid to make up for all the fun I would be missing that summer.

The man in the bike helmet accepted my proposal.

And I in turn accepted his acceptance. I took the job. It had fallen into my lap. I accepted it on philosophical grounds. I have a rule, as I've said, to accept the things that fall into my lap. I didn't tell him this, that my reasons for accepting were philosophical. He might have thought I was mentally ill.

I spent that summer mostly on my knees. It was hard work, but I found it enjoyable in a way. It's nice to build something. To watch it take shape. Something that wasn't there before.

It's funny how we spend our lives. Lifting stones, breaking rock, setting them into place. The wall gets built one stone at a time. Summer slips away. Slips right out from under us, whether we build something or not. No matter what we do. Autumn comes, leaves turn, anemones bloom. Then winter, anemones die back or die altogether. Then spring again. The wall will be there, but not everything will make it through.

Every Second Someone Dies

I was reading the book by the woman I love—my favorite female writer—she'd written about summer. She was alive in the book. Not dead yet, as she is now, as she has been for some time. She died over twenty-five years ago, in fact. I never knew her when she was alive. Meaning, I never read her books when she was alive. Not because she was alive, but because I didn't know who she was. I'd never heard of her.

That is the same with the man I love—my favorite male writer—who died five years later than the woman I love. I never knew him when he was alive either. Meaning . . . well, this isn't about him.

Or her.

Anyway, I was reading the book about summer by the woman I love. (I could say "by the woman whose books I love," but that wouldn't exactly describe how much she means to me.) It was morning. End of summer. September 8. I don't like even numbers. I remember at that point in my life, I had started reading in the mornings. I think because the summer nights stay light so long. I realized I wasn't reading at night, so I started getting up earlier in the morning, and reading.

I was reading her book about summer when I noticed the sun and the shadow on the book. The shadow from the window frame. That shadow was moving. I had the book perfectly still, and I could see the shadow moving. Not very fast, of course, but it was moving, and it was terrifying. She was describing the arc of her summer, and how it was ending, and it was very sad and beautiful. And I was reading it, and she was dead. Not only had her summer ended, but her life had ended. And my summer was ending, it was September 8 and the days were getting shorter. And I noticed the shadow on the page, and that it was moving.

I realized that, by watching that shadow, I was watching time move. I know this isn't that profound, but it struck me in a certain way. That morning. Time passing. I could see the end of all those seconds. I stared for minutes, no longer reading but watching the shadow move across the words, move across the words on the page. And something about the way the shadow moved across the words reminded me of those horrible WWII images of bodies being pushed into mass graves. The image just came to me, it wasn't my idea. And the shadow now seemed very sad. Very sad and frightening, but also beautiful, in a way, the way the shadow moved across the page. But I didn't want to find it beautiful. I'm not sure why. I didn't want to, but I couldn't help it.

CRICKET NEXT DOOR, I HEAR YOU OVER HERE

My friend Jason died. I know I've mentioned it before. I'm having a hard time getting over it. Or rather, getting through it. He drank himself to death. It's been a while since it happened. Ten years or more. But I only just found out about it recently. You see, it should've been me who died. I know that sounds cliché, and I apologize. But I was always the instigator, the one leading us down into the rings of hell. He Dante to my Virgil, if not the blind leading the blind. It certainly *could've* been me who died. It probably *should've* been me. I suppose it will be someday. I shouldn't be in such a hurry.

Our hellscape was the few years we spent together on the streets of New Orleans and elsewhere. We were teenagers. For three years we busked to buy whiskey and wine. Southern Comfort or jugs of Gallo. He played guitar. I improvised lyrics, kept rhythm with empty beer cans and garbage. The music was bad but that wasn't the point. We were alive and free and that was that. It was fantastic. It was our music.

We got into trouble together, and we kept each other safe.

After a few years, we lost track of each other. I was trying to get my life together and he just kept on in that life. When I found out he died, maybe twenty years after we'd lost touch, it hit me very hard. I learned every song I remembered him playing on the guitar. I sang them all. And for a few hours it felt like he was with me again, in the songs. I can pick up the guitar and bring him into the room like this. It's nice. And profoundly sad.

A couple of the songs are too intense to sing. He's too intensely present in them. "The Old Laughing Lady," and "Splendid Isolation." I can't sing those songs because I can't handle how completely I associate him with them. I can only hear his voice, see his gap-toothed smile, the dark nappy hair falling across his face. He had a beautiful voice that cracked when he reached for the high notes. Not a good voice, but a beautiful one. I'm sure I never told him that. We were eighteen, nineteen, twenty. I wish I'd taken the time, a few seconds only, to say "Hey, Jason, it's so fucking beautiful when you sing."

AT THE ORACLE

There were many times we went to the river. My friend Jason and I. This was in Indiana. Southern Indiana. The river was something like an oracle. Something to tell your secrets to, to wonder beside, to query.

I went back there a few years ago. After I found out he died. It was night. I sat on a huge log that had washed ashore, abandoned by a receding flood. Towboats still pushed barges of gravel and coal up and down the river, their bright spotlights searching the darkness for the banks.

At the oracle I was told I could ask one question. Only one. I tried to linger there, hoping I could somehow trick the universe. I offered it a hundred thousand ways of saying what this thing is we're in, this consciousness. I spoke in riddles or in short, declarative sentences. I mixed my metaphors or wove a web of rhetoric and implied response. I waxed poetic, or absurd. I'm sure I was offensive. I didn't care. I did whatever I could to get the oracle to reveal to me the nature of . . . well, nature. I did this as best I could without, technically, asking my question. Just saying it, sort of. Hoping for some recognition. I was saying around the bush.

I stayed there a long time. I still, sometimes, feel like I'm there, making offerings and questioning in my indirect way, my unquestioning way. I was making proposals, propositions. What for and why and to what purpose was this, I proposed.

The oracle was patient. The river flowed. What, after all, is time to oracles? It never answered my circuitous, perhaps too transparent attempts at outwitting it. It never answered the questions I never asked, though I tried my whole life to get a response.

Until finally, old and infirm, I confessed that I assumed, I proposed, hoped and wondered if one might live forever at the oracle. That is, if one might live forever at the oracle if you never finished your question. If you just kept asking it. Is that possible? I asked.

And, yawning, the oracle rolled its eyes and shook its head, then said clearly, in a voice dark and light and unforgiving, "no."

And then I had to leave.

Notes

iii **I condemn equally those who choose to praise**: the Pascal quote is from *Penseés*, pg. 146–7. The edition I use throughout is the Penguin Classics (1966).

iii **The story of my life does not exist**: the Duras quote is from her biography, *Marguerite Duras, A Life* (University of Chicago Press, 2000) by Laure Adler, trans. by Anne-Marie Glasheen, pg. 348.

ix **In every book the preface is**: Mihail Lermontov quotes are from his preface to *A Hero of Our Time* in the Nabokov translation (Anchor Books, 1958).

3 **Out of a hundred years**: Porchia quote from *Voices* (Copper Canyon, 2003)

6 **The swank of juvenile delinquency**: Fran Lebowitz's phrase in *The Fran Lebowitz Reader* (Vintage, 1994)

9 **As my dictionary says**: My dictionary is (still) the American Heritage College Dictionary (Third Edition, 1993). I'm not sure why I haven't updated to a more contemporary edition. Perhaps I'm not impressed with much of the new lexicon. In fact, I'm of the opinion that the older the dictionary, the more interesting it is.

27 **Oh Lord won't you buy me a night on the town**: from Janis Joplin's song, "Oh Lord."

29 **Mon frère, mon semblable**: "*mon semblable,—mon frère*" is from Baudelaire's poem "To the Reader" in *Flowers of Evil* (my edition is the Dover/Bantam, 1963).

30 **The bright clear days**: "The bright, clear days when she was with me, when we were together (without caring that we were together)." is taken from A.R. Ammons' poem "Nelly Myers" in his *Collected Poems 1951–1971* (Norton, 1972).

32 **What grape to keep its place in the sun**: the Connolly quote is from *The Unquiet Grave* (Persea, 2005).

64 **Curiosity is only vanity**: *Penseés*, pg. 50.

67 **One hair between them**: from Seng ts'an in *Cuckoo's Blood; Versions of Zen Masters*, by Stephen Berg (Copper Canyon, 2008).

73 **Wait, is Katy Perry the one who sings**: I've been advised that I need to make clear that "All I Wanna Do Is Have Some Fun" is a song by Sheryl Crow, and not Katy Perry.

74 **Telephones, and all the other agonies**: Cunningham quote is from a wall plaque at the Imogen Retrospective at Seattle Art Museum in 2021.

80 **Before the flowers of friendship faded**: Stein's "before the flowers of friendship faded, friendship faded," is the title of a book-length poem that she and Alice Toklas published. In 1930 the two of them started a literary press (Plain Edition) with the money they earned from selling Picasso's painting *Lady with a Fan* (1905). They published five books, all of them written by Stein.

87 **Don't say "fucking"**: In reality I never really cared much what type of language my daughter used, as long as it was appropriate to the situation. That aspect of parenting always seemed a bit hypocritical to me: the teaching of manners, polite language, and proper behavior. Maybe it's because, as a child, I had my mouth washed out with soap. Some behaviors are important, though, as when Duras says, "children should be taught three things: respect for their parents, respect for others, and not to cough in the theatre." (Adler, pg. 351)

93 **The writing is inevitably affected by the impatience of the medium**: Marguerite Duras, *Outside* (Beacon Press, 1986).

94 **Everything wrote when I was in the house writing**: from Adler's bio of Duras, pg. 386.

115 **Zen poems by Taigu Ryokan**: *One Robe, One Bowl: The Zen Poetry of Ryokan*, translated by John Stevens (Weatherhill, 11ᵗʰ edition, 1987).

120 **No Swan So Fine**: Moore's poem is found in *The Complete Poems of Marianne Moore* (Macmillan/Viking, 1980).

125 **Fame—the aggregate of all misunderstandings**: the Rilke epigraph is from *Letters*, but I've also found it at quotefancy.com superimposed on "wallpaper" of clouds reflected in a still pond(!).

126 **Fascism as a "healing agent"**: I don't mean to make too much of Rilke's quote about fascism as a "healing agent." From what I've read he seems to have written it a bit impulsively in a letter while he was staying in a sanatorium. It's also said that he was referring to the tonal qualities of fascist language as a kind of corrective, or that he was implying fascism is a correction of communism, etc. Whatever the reason for his statement, it's said that he immediately walked it back once the letter reached its target and that that target (Aurelia Gallaratti Scotti) became offended. My point is (if I must explain my point) that the New Age Community has no clue what it's putting on its meditation pillows, nor really cares, as long as they are selling. It is a capital-

ist movement that masquerades as spiritual at worst, a spiritual movement that embraces commodification at best.

127 **a mishappen Don Juan**: The word "mishappen" is arguably not a word at all. At least, it is a verb and I am (mis)using it as an adjective. I should note that both my wife and publisher object. They both corrected my usage to the word "misshapen." A *misshapen* Don Juan. But the Don Juan I am invoking is not an ill-constructed Mr. Potato Head. He's unlucky in love. He can't keep his foot out of his mouth. I suppose now that I think of it, someone with a foot in their mouth is ill-constructed after all . . .

171 **After Ryokan**: "After Ryokan" was written after a Ryokan poem (or an Ikkyu poem?) that I can no longer find. I've searched for hours but it seems the original has vanished. Or I've rewritten and revised the piece so many times that I no longer recognize its connection to the original . . . not uncommon for me I'm afraid.

177 **In lunatics the mouth is missing**: Jeanne Socquet quotes are from Duras' essay, "Socquet Jeanne" in *Outside* (Beacon Press 1984).

178 **The great lunacy of most lyric poems**: from Mary Ruefle's essay "Poetry and the Moon," in *Madness, Rack, and Honey* (Wave Books, 2012).

179 **The moon was the first poem**: ibid.

187 **For everything tends towards itself**: from Pascal's *Penseés*, pg. 154.

189 **That Shallow Brook**: the poet Mallarmé's phrase from his poem "Tombeau de Verlaine": *Un peu profond ruisseau calomnié la mort* (That shallow brook slandered, we call Death.)

197 **The void you discover in your teens**: from Marguerite Duras' *Practicalities* (Harper Collins, 1990).

208 **Real wisdom's when your dead twin suddenly walks up to you**: from Shenhui in *Cuckoo's Blood*.

208 **I believe that when I die I'll rot**: from Bertrand Russell's essay "Nature and Man," collected in *What I Believe* (1925). I heard Richard Dawkins quote it in an interview.

208 **The last act is bloody**: Pascal, *Penseés*, pg. 84.

214 **From now on**: the Issa quote is usually lineated: "From now on / it's all pure again / whatever it is" (Berg in *Cuckoo's Blood*).

219 **Cricket next door, I heard you over here**: a haiku by Issa (Berg in *Cuckoo's Blood*).

Thomas Walton's writing has appeared in numerous journals and magazines. He was founding editor of *PageBoy Magazine* (2005-2020) and is a contributing editor for *Exacting Clam*. He is grateful to have been nominated for the Pushcart Prize in both 2018 and 2022. As an undergraduate, Walton studied Russian and French Literature, and Puppetry, at The Evergreen State College. Upon graduating, he decided to engage in more practical pursuits, so enrolled in The Jack Kerouac School of Disembodied Poetics at Naropa University where he enjoyed sitting on cushions and walking along Boulder Creek.

Also by Thomas Walton

Good Morning Bone Crusher! (poems)
Spuyten Duyvil, 2021

All the Useless Things Are Mine (aphorisms)
Sagging Meniscus, 2020

The World Is All That Does Befall Us (essay)
Ravenna Press, 2019

with Elizabeth Cooperman:
The Last Mosaic (literary collage)
Sagging Meniscus, 2018

www.ingramcontent.com/pod-product-compliance
Lightning Source LLC
Chambersburg PA
CBHW031945010726
47493CB00007B/2089